A lazy, wi touched his mouth

"Shall I tell you what you remind me of?" he asked.

Louisa stiffened, her face tightening imperceptibly. "Go ahead," she said coolly, thinking he was going to insult her.

"You look like a royal princess," he told her softly, stroking her neck until he reached the leaping pulse in her throat. "A royal princess who's just stepped out of her lover's bed."

Louisa's breath caught in her throat. She stared at him with increasing excitement. "I am," she said softly.

He watched her, aware of the furious leap of her pulse at his words. His angular, hard-boned face was expressionless, his lithe body still, held in the grip of a powerful attraction.

"I see the illicit excites you," he drawled.

Louisa felt breathless, lightheaded. "Yes," she replied.

SARAH HOLLAND

fever pitch

Harlequin Books

TORONTO • NEW YORK • LOS ANGELES • LONDON
AMSTERDAM • PARIS • SYDNEY • HAMBURG
STOCKHOLM • ATHENS • TOKYO • MILAN

For
Debbie Seaman

Harlequin Presents first edition June 1983
ISBN 0-373-10601-7

Original hardcover edition published in 1983
by Mills & Boon Limited

CHAPTER ONE

LOUISA was in the middle of a conversation when she sensed it. She stiffened, frowning, her words trailing away into empty space. Bobby stood beside her, watching her, waiting for her to finish her sentence. But she didn't speak. Slowly she turned her head to look over her shoulder.

Then she saw him, his eyes gleaming in the darkness, two pinpoints of brilliant, predatory green light.

Her heart stopped with a thud, then quickened, her pulses leaping. There was something magnetic in that narrow-eyed stare, as though he knew her better than she knew herself, although they were total strangers. She held his gaze, her own eyes wide, dark and intense.

The pounding thud of the music fed into her bloodstream, the backdrop of incessant party chatter faded into the distance. Louisa had been alone for so long, distanced from her friends by an abyss which could never be crossed. Now fate was smiling on her, it had sent her a partner to fight the lonely hostile world with.

'Who is that man?' she asked under her breath, never taking her eyes off him.

Bobby peered across the room like a short-sighted owl. 'They call him Jacey,' he said into his glass. 'Don't know his real name.'

Jacey. His name was as unusual as he was. Louisa turned back to study him across the noisy heated room, and felt excitement throb in her bloodstream. It was a crazy, once-in-a-lifetime experience. The French called it *coup de foudre*, or struck by lightning. Italians called it the thunder-bolt. Louisa called it the most exhilarating, incredible feeling ever to move inside her.

Bobby was nursing his drink, his face owlish. 'Bit of a mystery man, really,' he continued. 'No one knows who he is or where he comes from. He just turns up out of the blue whenever he feels like it.'

They were watching each other, she and Jacey, eyes fever-bright, taking their time, knowing one another so totally that it was as though they could strip away the layers of skin and bone to reveal the raw strength beneath.

Louisa had never felt she belonged; she had always felt excluded, set apart, different. The stigma of her birth had locked into her soul, haunting her life, destroying her emotional contact with others. Illegitimacy was a frightening word to live with. But she knew that this man wouldn't care. She knew he would want her fiercely, the same way she wanted him. Destiny was drawing them together irrevocably.

'Shall I introduce you?' Bobby asked, seeing the rapid pulse that beat at her throat, the excitement in her flashing black eyes. 'You can't take your eyes off each other! Someone ought to put you both out of your misery!'

Louisa watched him laugh and felt her heart beat faster. 'That won't be necessary,' she murmured, almost unable to speak through her excitement. They would meet—in time.

Bobby seemed surprised, peering at her, brows raised, eyes wide. 'You're kidding!' His eyes flickered slightly in his surprise. 'You're almost eating each other across the room!'

It was true. But Louisa didn't want to meet him at a party with so many other people around, watching them. She wouldn't be able to relax, be able to be honest with him. This was so special, so intensely personal that she knew they had to meet alone, with no distractions, no complications. She could feel herself breathing rapidly, her heart hammering at her breastbone, and she didn't want to control it, didn't want to hide it. This was real and exciting. It showed in her eyes, the fever-bright sheen as she studied him.

She felt the crackle of frenetic energy inside her, because he smiled at her, and she felt her heart somersault so wildly that she had to look away in breathless confusion.

Bobby noticed. 'I see,' he said, grinning as she stared blankly at the wilting plant in the corner of the room. 'Not your type after all? That's a first! I shouldn't tell him, he might not like it!'

Louisa felt a secret smile touch her mouth. 'I don't think he'd give a damn,' she said under her breath.

Bobby's head swung to scrutinise Jacey. 'No,' he said wonderingly, 'I don't think he would.' He shook his head with amusement. 'He's an arrogant bastard.'

No, thought Louisa, he's not arrogant. He's just strong. In the same way that I am—because life gave us no other choice. In this world you either get the role of victim or hunter—unless you're born with a silver spoon in your mouth. You're either a winner or a loser. And Louisa had been a loser, and a victim, all her life until three years ago. Then she had made a conscious decision—no one was ever going to beat her again. And no one ever had.

She kept her thoughts and feelings hidden behind a mask. No one saw behind her face into her mind. No one saw into her heart. She'd learned early that when you're vulnerable you get attacked, and she'd been hurt too many times to leave herself open to attack.

She turned to Bobby with a warm smile. 'I'd better be off now.' She put her drink down on the mantel, her eyes flickering with restless thoughts. 'I'll see you at work on Monday.'

Bobby made a face. 'Party pooper! It's only midnight.' He sighed, 'Well, I suppose you know best. But get an early night tomorrow—you know you always look dead on Monday mornings!'

Louisa smiled and gave him a pat on the head. 'See you!'

The man called Jacey watched her as she left the room. She felt his eyes searing into her back, and as she reached the door, she turned. Their eyes met and she read the signal in his with a leap of excitement. He would follow—when he was ready.

Other pairs of eyes watched as she passed, paying homage to her beauty.

Even at a distance, Louisa Faulkner was breathtaking. The huge flashing black eyes dominated a face with regal bone structure that was strikingly beautiful. Cascades of midnight black hair slid around her shoulders to draw attention to her sensual but elegant body.

She left the noise and heat of the party behind her, walking slowly into the crisp winter air, alone in the night. London watched her silently as she walked, regarding her with an air of detached interest.

She heard the door of the house swing open, the noise escaping for a moment. Then the door closed and she listened to the cool click of his heels as he came after her.

He caught up with her, his long legs unhurried as he reached her side. She felt her nerve-endings crackle at his presence.

'You should have waited for me,' he said, sliding an amused glance at her from those panther-green eyes.

A smile touched her full pink mouth. 'Should I ?' she murmured, without looking at him.

'I might not have followed you,' he pointed out coolly as they turned the white stone corner, walking beneath a golden street lamp.

'Then,' said Louisa quietly, 'you wouldn't have been worth waiting for.'

He stopped walking, and studied her. Then he laughed softly under his breath, watching her in an electric silence. The chill wind blew a strand of her hair across her face, a taxi could be heard in another street, its engine distant.

'What's your name?' he asked softly.

'Louisa.'

He raised one dark brow. 'Sounds Latin,' he murmured, and the breeze ruffled his thick black hair. He raked a hand through it silently, pushing it back over his tanned forehead. 'And do you live up to it?' His smile was crooked, amused. 'Are you hot-blooded and intense?'

She studied him for a long moment, aware of his strength in every nerve-ending in her body. What she was experiencing seemed so impossible, and yet so totally real.

'Yes,' she said slowly, and a smile touched her mouth, 'I live up to my name.'

He considered her with those brilliant green eyes, the sooty lashes resting on his tanned cheek. 'I believe you do.' A lazy, wicked smile touched his mouth. 'Shall I tell you what you look like? What you remind me of?'

Louisa stiffened, her face tightening imperceptibly. 'Go ahead,' she said coolly, waiting in case he was going to insult her. Could she have been wrong about him?

'You look like a royal princess,' he told her softly, and one long finger stroked her neck until it reached the leaping pulse in her throat. 'A royal princess who's just stepped out of her lover's bed.'

Her breath caught in her throat. She stared at him with increasing excitement, then she felt a soft laugh touch her throat, and she smiled at him.

'I am,' she said softly.

He watched her in silence, noting the furious leap of her pulses at his words. The angular, hard-boned face was expressionless, his lithe body still, held in the grip of a powerful attraction.

'I see the illicit excites you,' he drawled, and one dark brow rose as he waited for her reply.

She felt breathless, lightheaded. 'Yes.'

He smiled into the silence, his eyes sliding over her body. 'No coat?' He raised one brow as he studied her short black dress. 'That's a beautiful dress, but aren't you cold?'

'A little.' The cold couldn't touch her tonight. She was almost walking on air. She didn't own a coat, couldn't afford one, and usually had to suffer for it. But not tonight. The magic would keep her warm tonight.

'I'm not usually so gallant,' Jacey said smokily, and his eyes glinted as he slid his jacket off, 'but I wouldn't be a gentleman if I didn't offer you mine.'

Louisa raised one brow in seductive challenge. 'You don't look like a gentleman to me,' she said softly.

He stopped, making her heart skid, and leaned towards her, holding the collar of the jacket beneath her chin.

'I'm not,' he murmured huskily.

Louisa shivered as his hands slid from her throat over her shoulders and down her arms in a deliberately sensual movement. She couldn't move because her heart wouldn't let her, it was thumping too fast.

He caught her hand in his. 'Let's walk,' he said softly, then smiled.

They walked around London for the rest of the night. Occasionally they stopped, going into all-night cafés, sitting across from one another drinking black coffee and talking. Talking endlessly, discovering each other, reaching each other. And as they talked, they fell deeper and deeper in love until Louisa wondered how she had ever existed without him.

Her feet ached from walking, her throat dry from talking, but still she walked by his side, her hand in his, talking animatedly, her excitement growing by the minute.

'London at dawn,' Jacey commented as they walked beside the walls of Buckingham Palace. The streets were crisp, silent. Distant sounds of life were beginning to be heard as the occasional car drove along. 'Beautiful, isn't it? It always makes me feel more optimistic to wait up at dawn and see the city come alive.'

She tilted her head to look at him with a curious smile. 'Does it?'

He nodded, smiling. 'It's easier to believe in tomorrow if you see it born.' He raised her hand to his mouth and pressed his firm lips against it, the gesture at once both intensely sexy and tender. 'Watching life begin again proves that you can always make a new start, try again.'

Louisa smiled into his eyes. 'I've never looked at it like that before.' The truth in his statement had reached her, made her think. She was beginning to realise that he had incredible depth, that everything he said was thought-provoking.

Jacey stopped, leaning lazily against the cold brick walls of the Palace gardens. 'No matter how many times you get knocked down, you always have to get up again,' he said gently, and smiled. 'People are always going to kick your face in, whatever you try to do to stop them. You just have to keep on smiling, keep on picking yourself up off the floor.'

Their hands slid together in a heartfelt caress, and Louisa smiled with her soul. 'I wish we'd met a long time ago,' she said, laughing lightheartedly.

He frowned, curious. 'Why? What happened a long time ago?'

She sighed, avoiding his eyes for a moment. How did you tell a man you were falling hopelessly in love with that you were illegitimate? Easy, she thought sadly, just say it. I'm illegitimate. But she wasn't ready. She couldn't hand him her soul on a plate.

'When I first left home,' she said slowly, 'I came here, to the West End. I was seventeen, I had no money, no friends, and nowhere to go. I slept rough that first night, and when I woke up it was dawn.' She shuddered at the memory and looked across at Jacey. 'London looked cold and hostile, and I hated it. It made me feel empty . . . empty and numb.'

Jacey frowned, his dark brows linking. 'That was dangerous, wasn't it?'

She laughed softly, looking at him with sad eyes. 'What else could I do? London is unkind to strangers with no money.'

He tilted his dark head to one side. 'But you don't have a London accent.'

She shook her head. 'Cultivated. I was born in the East End.' Her smile was dry, her brows raised. 'It's a world apart, believe me. I had to drop it in order to hold down a job.'

Jacey nodded, looking down at her and Louisa's pulses leapt crazily The excitement was crackling between them. She had never felt anything so powerful, so intense before.

'Hungry?' he asked huskily.

She nodded, breathless, her throat tight. 'Very.'

He smiled slowly, and she almost swayed against him. 'Good. I know a lovely little place near here—not too expensive, but the food's good.'

She groaned, laughing. 'Not another of your little cafés!'

Jacey caught her hand, grinning. 'And why not?'

Their eyes met in a riveting caress, and Louisa felt as though all the breath had been knocked out of her. She couldn't move, couldn't speak. She was afraid to break the spell.

She stared at him intensely. Then she said, 'I don't think I could eat a thing.'

Jacey was totally still for a moment, then he slowly took her hand and pressed it to his tightly muscled chest until she felt the deep thud of his heart that matched her own.

'I know,' he said simply. Then he smiled, and they walked in silence to Park Lane.

They ate in a little café on Park Lane, sitting by the window, watching London come alive. Louisa felt she had known Jacey for as long as she had known herself. There was a magical honesty between them.

'So when did you leave home?' Jacey asked, sipping coffee from an earthen brown mug.

Louisa dropped her gaze to her own coffee. 'Three years ago,' she said huskily. A part of her wanted desperately to tell him the truth about her background. But she decided against it. That could wait. Smiling, she looked back at him. 'How about you?'

He laughed, exposing sharp white teeth. He rested his chin in one lean tanned hand, his face thoughtfully amused. 'Well, I'm thirty-six now, so it must have been eighteen years ago.' His eyes rested on her face. 'Does that make me sound very old?' he asked gently.

'You're as old as you feel.' She sipped her steaming coffee, smiling at him. It didn't matter a damn to her how old he was. *He* mattered to her, and that was all that counted.

He considered her with panther-green eyes. 'How true,' he agreed. He placed his hand over hers and an electric shock ran through her. 'I think we go well together, Louisa,' he said deeply.

'Yes,' she said breathlessly.

Her life changed overnight. Before she met him her world had been empty and sad, she had been isolated, alone. No one had reached her, no one had pierced the core of her loneliness, come close to the reality of her character.

Now at last she had found someone who understood without being told, who could see behind the defences behind the cool mask to the real Louisa. He wasn't fooled by the self-confident air she fought desperately to keep, he saw she was vulnerable, alone, and he saw how much she needed him.

In her turn, Louisa saw behind his defences too. She saw behind the fleshless hard-boned face to the strength inside him, saw the burning intelligence in his brilliant green eyes, saw the warmth and tenderness which went hand in hand with his strength.

She saw herself in him and knew they were perfectly matched.

'Are you sure he's right for you?' Bobby's worried voice came from behind the counter at the bookshop where they worked. Louisa could just see the top of his sandy head bobbing about behind it as he stamped prices on books.

'I'm sure,' she said lightly.

Bobby peered at her over the counter. 'Listen, I know you're a tough cookie, you can take care of yourself, but——' he sighed, 'well, no one knows anything about him. He could be anyone.'

She eyed him. 'No, he couldn't,' she said softly. 'He could only ever be Jacey.'

She stopped what she was doing and put the

books down. She knew all she needed to know about Jacey. They were two of a kind—restless, haunted spirits who were strong enough to look out for themselves, but needed each other just the same.

Bobby stood up from the floor, dusting the knees of his old blue suit. 'You will be careful, won't you? You hardly know him.'

She laughed softly. 'I have been seeing him for over a month, Bobby.'

Bobby grunted irritably. 'A month! That isn't long enough. For all you know he could be Bluebeard with six dead wives locked in the attic.'

Her cheeks dimpled. 'He hasn't got an attic, Bobby!'

But it wasn't that. She knew Jacey better than she knew herself. They were soulmates, shaped in the same way by similar knocks, their characters slotting together like two halves of a jigsaw puzzle.

The bell jangled as the shop door opened. Louisa looked up, and her heart thudded faster as she saw the familiar dark figure walk in casually, closing the door behind him.

'Hello,' Jacey said smokily, walking over to where she stood.

She stepped down from the ladder, her breathing quickening. 'What brings you here?' she asked huskily. No matter how many times she saw him his impact always made her whole body jangle with excitement.

He smiled and her heart skipped a beat. 'You,' he murmured. He looked dangerously sexy in black jeans and a black sweater. 'I've got the afternoon off,' he said, sliding his hands into the pockets of his jeans. 'I thought maybe you could too.'

Bobby was glowering, listening to them. 'Scotty won't like it,' he said, glaring at Jacey.

Jacey raised one dark brow. 'Why do I get the feeling he doesn't like me?' he drawled lazily. He leaned against the bookshelves, folding his arms and watching Bobby with amusement.

Bobby looked very cross. His ears went pink. 'All right,' he muttered, slamming books, 'take the afternoon off. But you can explain to Scotty in the morning, because I'm not going to.'

Jacey pushed away from the shelves lazily, and Louisa felt her breath catch. 'Ready?' he asked.

They went to his flat on the other side of town. It was too far to walk, so they caught a bus, sitting on the top deck, looking out of the window as they laughed over Bobby's behaviour. Louisa told him what Bobby had said before he came into the shop.

Jacey's eyes narrowed as he looked down at her. 'Does it matter to you?' he asked seriously. 'Would you prefer to know more about me? About my background?'

Louisa shook her head. 'It's not important. Besides,' her face sobered, guilt surfacing inside her, 'you know very little about me either.'

Jacey eyed her silently. Then he looked up. 'Come on!' He caught her hand as the bus veered unsteadily around a corner. 'Our stop.'

They raced down the steps, their feet clattering, and leapt off the bus as it pulled away from the stop, landing unsteadily on the pavement. Jacey took her hand as they started to walk along the leafy back street towards his small flat.

Louisa had been surprised when he first took her to his flat. It was in a terraced house, run by

an old landlady who complained and moaned
every time she saw Jacey. The flat itself was small,
cramped and badly furnished, obviously very
cheap.

'I don't need money,' Jacey had told her when
she asked why he lived in such a ramshackle place
at his age. 'It just gets in the way, stops you being
yourself.'

Now, they walked into the musty old house
while the landlady, Mrs Martin, poked her
withered nose around the door, clutching her worn
cardigan to her spindly body.

'No mud on them shoes, I hope?' Mrs Martin
eyed Jacey's feet suspiciously.

'On a day like this?' Jacey replied with a smile as
they closed the door behind them.

Mrs Martin sniffed. 'Gets into my bones, this
wind. I wish summer would hurry up.' She pushed
her spectacles higher on the bony bridge of her
nose.

Jacey grinned as they walked to the stairs. 'But
you know how you hate the heat. You told me last
year it made you feverish.'

Mrs Martin sighed wearily. 'You're right,
you're right. It's my punishment for being old,
God help me.' She shook her head and shuffled
off into her own rooms, while Jacey led the way
upstairs.

'One of life's complainers,' Jacey remarked as
they went up the creaking stairs to his rooms at
the top of the house. He laughed, opening the
door and going into the cramped living room.
'Like your friend Bobby.'

Louisa smiled, sitting down on the ragged
armchair. 'You mustn't take any notice of him,

Jacey.' She smiled up at him, eyes dancing. 'It's just because you're so different.'

One dark brow rose with amusement. 'Different?'

She nodded. 'Well, you are thirty-six, and you have no roots, no particular ambitions.'

His face hardened, and Louisa was surprised, watching his mouth firm, his eyes darken.

'True,' he said curtly, and the green eyes held an angry glitter that disturbed her. 'I did have once. In fact I was very ambitious at one time.' He smiled coldly. 'A regular whizz-kid, putting dynamite under companies and turning the losers into winners.'

She frowned, watching him. 'What happened?'

Again, his mouth firmed angrily. 'I got sick of it.' The deep anger in his voice made her stare at him, amazed, seeing the change in him, the icy contempt in his eyes. He crossed to the tiny window, staring out of it with a brooding expression. 'Something happened to make me want to get out of the whole damned-jungle. I used to wake up and see what I had to live with.' His eyes darkened, narrowing. 'It made me want to throw up.'

Louisa was silent for a long time. She didn't know what to say. It was the first inkling she had ever had of a stormy past he might be hiding from her.

She moistened her lips and asked, 'Do you want to tell me about it? It might help.'

Jacey looked over his shoulder with grim amusement. 'Help?' He laughed. 'If I couldn't help myself, what makes you think you could? It would make me physically sick to go back to that world. I've left it all behind me now.'

She stiffened, horrified to find herself putting a mask over her face to conceal the sudden pain she felt inside at his rejection. It was the first time he'd ever rejected her, and to do it so coldly was like a nail being driven through her heart.

'You shouldn't lock things inside, Jacey,' she told him coolly, again horrified by the way she was hiding her true feelings from him.

He just looked at her, his face immovable.

She felt angry. 'Would you rather I wasn't interested?'

He studied her, the line of cheek and jaw harsh. 'Frankly, yes.'

Louisa could feel her face tighten as she stared at him. Resentment burnt inside her as they watched each other silently across the worn furniture, their faces hostile.

There should be no secrets, she thought angrily. And yet she had told him very little about herself either. But in holding back she had felt no seeds of doubt—she had just thought the time wasn't right. Now she could feel the doubt eating into her stomach like a cancer.

'Was what happened so terrible,' she asked through barely parted lips, 'that you can't even bring yourself to tell me?'

Jacey nodded, eyes narrowed.

Her eyes searched his deeply. 'Why, Jacey?' she asked in a low voice.

He swung on her, eyes leaping. 'Leave it!' he muttered through his teeth, and she jerked away in shock at the expression on his face.

'I will!' she retorted angrily, standing up and moving to the door.

But he was faster. His hand shot out to grip her

wrist, jerking her back towards him. 'What the hell are you doing?' he muttered under his breath.

'What does it look like?' she snapped back.

Jacey was silent for a long time, studying her intently. It was as though he was searching deep into her mind, trying to get inside her head, although there was no need for it. She would let him in any time he wanted. All he had to do was ask.

'You worry me, Louisa,' he said eventually. 'You're so ambitious, so angry with the world. It'll destroy you in the end.'

'If you don't like the way I am, Jacey, you can take a running jump!'

He eyed her, his mouth hard. 'I can understand why you feel like that. You've had a rough time, you want to hit out at life. But you can't. If you try, life will hit you back, twice as hard.'

Her eyes flashed a deep angry black. 'I'm me, Jacey,' she said under her breath, her body tense. 'Take me or leave me.'

There was a tense silence, then he reached out one hand to slide sensually over her throat, his fingers thrusting in her thick black hair.

'I think I'll take you,' he muttered, drawing her closer.

The weeks slipped by, but the incident didn't fade in her mind. It had been their first argument, and she wasn't ready to forget it. Louisa recognised a milestone when she saw one.

Before, when she had argued with boy-friends, the feelings had been mainly irritation, annoyance, as though she hadn't really wanted to bother with arguing. But Jacey was different, so different. Her feelings had been so intense, so violent, and the fact that she was falling more and more in love with him frightened her. How could she feel this much for one human being?

'I'll make an honest woman of you one day,' Jacey told her as they walked hand in hand across Hyde Park one Sunday morning. The grass was damp beneath their feet, the air crisp, the chill winter sunshine cool.

'Oh?' Louisa turned to look at him, brows raised. 'Am I dishonest?' and those panther green eyes burnt into her, making her heart thud faster with what she saw in them.

The need for each other was eating away at both of them, working up to fever pitch. The longer she denied him, the more she wanted him. It was becoming almost unbearable to stand too close to him because their awareness of each other was ferocious, tangible.

Her mouth dried up every time she caught a glimpse of his tanned flesh, her heart rocketed every time he kissed her. She was a walking time-bomb, constantly aroused, constantly needing him. It would only take one touch to make her explode.

But she was afraid. At first it had been fear of losing him. Now it was fear of giving herself totally to a man who was secretive. How could she be sure that he wouldn't leave her if she made love to him?

Yet it was also fear of her own feelings. She sensed that when they did finally make love, it would be a cataclysmic explosion for them both. And the longer it went unsated, the more explosive it became. She felt as though their bodies were turning into animals with their violent need of each other.

'Here,' Jacey reached into his coat pocket with one hand, 'present for you.'

'A present?' Her face lit up, and she laughed. 'I like presents. Is it a box of chocolates?' But then he held out his hand, and her breath got stuck in the back of her throat as she saw the sunlight reflect and glitter in solid gold rays. 'Wow!' she whispered, staring.

'He's called Bubo,' Jacey said lazily, holding the gold statuette up to the sun. 'He was Athena's owl.'

But she was staring at the exquisite golden owl with a cold taste of fear in her mouth. 'Jacey . . .' she said on a whisper, 'it's beautiful—but where on earth did you get it? It must have cost a small fortune!' Her eyes raised to his face, wide and haunted with fear. 'You don't have that kind of money.'

'See his eyes?' Jacey pointed to the black stones. 'They're like yours—very black, very wise. I think you were born wise. The angels whispered secrets to you before you were born.'

Her gaze flickered restlessly. 'Jacey,' she said, swallowing, 'Jacey, where did you get it?'

He was silent and still. He watched her, his face brooding, and she saw the mask slide into place, leaving a hostile dangerous stranger in place of the man she loved.

'Does it matter?' he asked curtly.

Louisa frowned. She wasn't used to backing down; it went against her inbuilt sense of self-preservation. But she could see plainly that he wouldn't tell her where he got the statuette. This once, she thought angrily. This once I shall back down.

'It doesn't matter,' she said, but her voice belied her words.

It mattered, and he knew it. But it was the fact that he wouldn't tell her where he'd got the money that made her angry—and that was different.

A mystery man, Bobby had said. Bobby had known what he was talking about. Jacey kept his past locked securely in the past, and he didn't want her to tamper with the lock.

Who are you? she thought intently, but she already knew. He was ready to hand her his raw self, but the life he'd led bevore didn't come part and parcel with it. She had to accept what he was ready to give.

'Don't you want it?' Jacey's voice was cold, his eyes narrowed as he held out the golden owl.

She looked at it for a long time. Then, 'Thank you,' she said slowly, and held out her own hand. It was an olive branch and she grasped it, holding on tightly to what she was so sure was hers.

He belonged to her and she wasn't letting go without a fight. Even if it meant she would lose some of her own self-respect in the process, even if it meant compromise after compromise in the process.

'He's everything you want, is he?' old Mr Scott asked one afternoon as they cashed up at the end of the day.

Louisa raised her head. 'Yes,' she said, eyeing the top of his greying head, 'I think so.'

But she wasn't so sure. Jacey was everything she wanted in a man, but although her life was richer

now than it had ever been, she felt a sense of
dissatisfaction with life outside Jacey.

Maybe she expected too much of him. Maybe
she was too easily hurt. Or maybe she needed
something else. Maybe she needed more than
Jacey. But did that mean Jacey wasn't right for
her? She sighed, shaking her head.

There were more questions than answers.

But what if she married him? For the first few
weeks, every time they made love it would be with
violent emotion, with the ferocity of animals. But
after that—what then? The intensity of their love
might fade, and what would she be left with? She
would have no life of her own outside Jacey. And
she knew now that she needed a life of her own,
apart from him, but with him.

Mr Scott's eyes were kind. 'You have to be
sure,' he told her gently, and his withered hand
stopped, resting on the receipts he was leafing
through. 'It's painful to make mistakes—especially
the marrying kind.'

Louisa stiffened. 'I realise that,' she said coolly,
her face smoothing over. 'I have to make my own
mistakes, though.' She turned back to the adding
machine in front of her, her fingers working
quickly.

Scotty was silent for a moment. Then he stood
up, his face wrinkled in a frown. 'I'm a nosey old
devil, I know,' he said kindly, and his watery blue
eyes searched hers. 'Doesn't do to poke your nose
in where it's not wanted, but ...' he sighed,
shaking his head.

She gave him a polite smile. 'But it's for my own
good?'

He nodded slowly. 'Aye, lassie, it's for your own

good.' He eyed her sadly, then smiled. 'I wouldn't want to see you get hurt. Not after you've been strong for so long.'

Louisa bent her head, ashamed. Scotty was her oldest ally in London. He had been the first person to treat her with kindness, and she should have treated him with a lot more respect.

'I'm sorry,' she said huskily, looking up at him, eyes troubled. She knew he had only been worried for her and it was time she remembered just how much she owed him. More than she could ever repay.

The telephone bell shrilled into the silence. Scotty grimaced, picking it up and muttering into it hurriedly.

'For you.' He waved the receiver and smiled. 'Jacey.'

She felt the familiar thud of her heart and reached out for the phone with a smile in her voice as she said, 'Hallo.'

'Something's come up.' Jacey's voice was cool and impersonal and Louisa frowned, wondering what had happened. 'I won't be able to make it tonight.'

She felt her heart sink with disappointment at his words. 'Why not?' she asked—but she should have known better.

There was a pause. 'I can't tell you, Louisa,' he said in a low voice, and her frown deepened with a sense of disbelief. She waited to hear if there was more, but he was silent.

Louisa took a deep breath. 'When will I see you?' She hated herself for it, because it sounded so much as though she was begging for his time, but she couldn't help herself. She had to know.

'Soon.' Jacey's voice was warm and she felt relief flood through her. 'I'll call you when I get back.'

Louisa jerked back in shock as the line went dead. She stared at the receiver for a full minute before she realised he had actually hung up on her without saying goodbye.

Slowly she replaced the receiver, her face white. She felt very cold inside, as though a premonition had been ignored and now time was catching up with her.

'Is anything wrong?' Scotty was watching her, his straggly grey brows linked in a frown of concern.

Louisa stared at the wall with unseeing black eyes. 'No . . .' she murmured, her voice distracted, her body still.

But she knew it was a lie— something was going wrong between her and Jacey, and she was powerless to prevent it.

She didn't hear from him for three days. The silence was almost unbearable for her, punctuated with shattered hopes every time the telephone rang, every time the door opened for a customer. She would look up quickly, Jacey's figure in her mind's eyes, and see a stranger, and then her heart would hurt with disappointment.

He was necessary to her—she saw that now, with painful clarity. Just three days, and she felt as though her whole world had fallen apart. When they had first met she had simply been over-whelmed with intense emotion for him, pleased that fate had sent her a partner who was so much like herself.

Now she knew she desperately needed him, and

that was quite different. But why was he so secretive? she asked herself as she lay awake in bed one night, staring into the blank darkness. The secrets will destroy us, she thought angrily—surely he must realise that?

Her pride was steadily being eaten away by a need to get inside his head. She had been so sure they were alike, two of a kind. But, she asked herself, would one of my own kind destroy my self-respect?

Love, she thought, and laughed out loud, angrily. Loving Jacey had changed her drastically. She had been strong, and now she was weak. She had been self-sufficient, and now she clung to him. She almost hated herself for it.

She had heard a song that day which had jolted her. Listening to the lyric, she had felt her mouth tighten angrily. It was about someone who looked into the mirror and saw someone they didn't want to be. And that was how she felt.

I don't want to be such a fool, she thought angrily. I want to be me again, to think for myself instead of needing Jacey with me all the time. He had turned her into a dull shadow.

Some time in the night, she jerked awake. Blinking back the sleep, she stared into the silent darkness, wondering what had woken her. Then she heard it again.

A stone clattered on to the window next to her, falling back to the ground with a hollow thud. She sat up, her heart hammering as she reached to pull the curtains back.

'Louisa!' Jacey's whisper reached her ears as she looked out into the street.

Her fingers didn't work properly as she pulled

the window up and looked out. 'Do you know what time it is?' she asked breathlessly. Her pulses were going haywire, thudding crazily at the sight of him. She could barely speak, her mind not working properly, forgetting all her doubts and self-searching.

Jacey grinned. 'Three o'clock. Let me in.'

She laughed, feeling a bubble of relief in her throat. He had come back for her. Jumping out of bed, she pulled her wrap on shakily, jerking it together at the waist and hurrying downstairs.

Jacey lounged against the doorjamb. 'Good morning,' he said smokily as she opened the door. His eyes burnt over her slender body in the thin white wrap. 'You look good enough to eat.'

Louisa laughed huskily. 'I am.' Holding the door back, she felt breathless, the impact of his dark good looks devastating her. 'Come in. You'll wake my landlord up if you stand there much longer.'

He pushed away from the door and came in lazily, standing in front of her in the hall. The silence was fraught with tension as they watched each other, and Louisa was sure he must be able to hear her heart thudding.

'Are we going to stand here all night?' he murmured, sliding one hand over her waist and drawing her towards him.

Louisa felt the touch with a ripple of sensuality that made her pulses drum crazily inside her. She slid one hand over his brown throat and strained against him, her face alight with hunger and need.

'Why did you stay away so long?' she asked throatily, hardly able to speak.

He studied her silently for a moment. 'Questions,

questions,' he said huskily, then his head bent slowly, and his warm firm mouth was moving over hers until she almost whimpered. He drew away, flushed, breathing hard. 'Let's go up,' he muttered thickly, and they went up to her flat in silence, while he followed her into the living room.

Jacey eyed her with a lazy smile. 'Missed me?' he asked deeply.

Her pulses leapt with the same old excitement. She smiled, her eyes dancing. 'Didn't give you a thought!' she lied, her cheeks dimpling.

Jacey's brows rose. 'Is that so?' he drawled, walking towards her, his hard mouth curving in a smile. One hand slid over hers, the long fingers curling on her wrist. 'I thought of you all the time. I can see I haven't made much of an impact on you.' His green eyes darkened. 'I shall have to try harder. I wouldn't want you to forget me.'

She started to smile, but the words got through to her, and her smile wavered. 'Forget you?' she queried, her voice uncertain. 'Why should I do that?'

Jacey studied her for a long moment in silence. The smile left his face, and she saw the brooding expression slip into place, his mouth firming, his expression serious.

'Jacey?' Her whole body was stiff, icy cold with fear as she watched him. She laughed nervously, her eyes darting over him. 'Why should I forget you, Jacey?'

His hand slid away from hers, dropping to his side. He gave a harsh sigh, raking his fingers through his black hair as he turned his back to her, his broad shoulders held in tension.

Louisa was really worried now. 'Jacey,' her

voice was low with fear as she laid a hand on his arm, 'tell me what's going on!'

There was a tense silence, then he said deeply, 'I have to go away for a while.'

She stared at him. He had only just come back. Swallowing, she said, 'How long is a while?'

He shrugged broad shoulders, the muscles rippling powerfully beneath his dark jacket. 'A month, maybe two.'

Her heart stopped beating. 'Two months?' she asked, dry-mouthed.

He thrust his hands into his pockets. Louisa noticed for the first time that he was dressed in black, his suit exquisitely cut, obviously expensive. 'Where did you get that suit?' she asked, eyeing it, a premonition of fear gripping her suddenly. 'I haven't seen it before.'

Jacey ignored the question. 'Will you wait for me?' His eyes were intense as he watched her. 'I don't know when I'll be back, I can't give any guarantees. But I want you to wait for me.'

Louisa smiled nervously. 'Of course I will,' she said, and she felt her heart beating in a slow deathly rhythm. 'But why don't you take me with you? Surely that would be easier?'

His face hardened. 'I can't,' he said abruptly. He walked slowly away to the other side of the room, stopping by the mantel to pick up little ornaments and finger them absently.

'Well, at least tell me where you're going,' she urged, keeping her voice as controlled as possible while she watched his brooding face.

Jacey shook his head. 'I can't do that either.' He looked across at her stricken face, and sighed harshly. 'I'm sorry, Louisa. Maybe when I get back I'll feel up to it.'

'Maybe when you get back . . .?' she whispered, struggling for self-control. She couldn't believe this was happening. The earth between them was splitting apart, and a great abyss was yawning, ready to destroy them. She had never felt so desperately lost in her life.

Jacey came towards her, his face dark and brooding. 'All I can do is ask you to trust me,' he said deeply, and his hands slid to hers, holding them gently.

Louisa lost control. 'Trust you?' she echoed angrily. 'How can I do that? You tell me you're going away, you won't say where or why, and you won't say when you're coming back— and you ask me to *trust* you?' Her eyes flashed an angry black. 'What is there to trust?'

His face hardened. 'Me. That should be enough for you.'

She laughed angrily. 'Oh, thanks a lot! I'm supposed to be grateful for the crumbs you throw me, am I?'

Jacey's hands slid to her shoulders, the long fingers tightening on her. 'You're too proud, Louisa,' he said in a low voice. 'If your pride can get in the way of your feelings, then your feelings can't be very strong.'

She pulled away from him, her heart thudding fast as she struggled for self-control. He was right, and she knew it, but her pride was strong and she couldn't throw away her self-respect.

'And neither can yours,' she flung back at him. 'You hide behind lies and secrets—how can I get close to you if you permanently push me away?'

His eyes leapt with anger. 'I asked you a long

time ago if my past mattered to you. You knew what you were getting into right from the start. Don't start trying to hit out at me for it now.'

She stared at him bitterly. 'I wish I'd never met you,' she said through her teeth.

His eyes were filled with violence for a moment. The silence between them was intense and deadly. Then he straightened, his face an angry mask as he watched her with narrowed eyes.

'The feeling,' he said bitingly, 'is mutual.'

He turned on his heel and strode out of the room, leaving the door swinging behind him.

Louisa stood in stunned disbelief, listening to the click of his heels as he left the flat, going out into the night.

CHAPTER TWO

LIFE without Jacey was a day-after-day torment for Louisa. She saw his face in her mind everywhere she went. Passing places where they had spent time together made her hurt inside, as her mind conjured up vivid images of what they had shared.

Friends were sympathetic when they noticed that she was no longer spending her time with Jacey. But they weren't surprised. He had always been a mystery to them, and his disappearances were usual.

After a fortnight of agony, Louisa threw her pride to the winds and telephoned everyone she knew, trying to find out if they knew where he was. No one had any idea.

Scotty watched her sadly, almost as though he could feel what she was going through. But he said nothing, trying to keep her mind off Jacey as much as possible.

'Maybe he'll come back,' said Scotty one day as he noticed her staring into space, her face tight with pain.

Louisa shook her head slowly. 'No,' she said, hurting inside, 'he'll never come back.'

Everything reminded her of him. Every song she heard conjured up his face. The radio played constantly in the little bookshop where she worked, and the words of one particular song made her wince.

'. . . All dressed in black, he won't be coming back . . .' was a lyric that haunted her for days, going round and round in her head, constantly on her lips.

Then, a month after Jacey had left, something happened to change her life. It seemed so ordinary at the time, but it overturned her life completely.

She was stamping prices on a pile of books when she became aware of being watched. Her gaze flickered a little and she realised someone was leaning on the counter, watching her.

'Hi,' said a deep male voice.

Louisa looked up into dancing blue eyes. He wore a red leather jacket, faded blue jeans and a cheeky amused expression as though he was making a judge or pillar of society stamp around and make a fool of himself. His face was long and thin and his hair spiky blond and tousled.

He grinned at her. 'Did you know you could get stamper's elbow doing that?'

'Really?' she said in a polite little voice.

'Oh yes,' he said gravely, but his lips tried to smile. 'Rare disease, but it plays havoc with your love life.'

Louisa's smile disappeared. 'Can I help you?' she asked coldly.

He coughed selfconsciously. 'Er—I was looking for a book on Musicians of the Seventies—you know, rock and roll, etc.' He gave her a quick uncertain smile. 'Got anything along that line?'

Louisa pointed to a row of books. 'The Musical section is over there.'

He nodded, and walked slowly over to the section. Louisa noted the worn, rather tatty sneakers he wore with his faded denims. She bent her head and continued pricing the books.

The man came back, offered her a book and paid for it, watching her as she slipped it into a paper bag with a polite, neutral expression.

'What are you doing tonight?' he asked suddenly as she handed him the book.

Crying, thought Louisa. But she replied coolly, 'Taking my pet alligator for a walk.'

He laughed, his eyes creasing with delight. 'I like you,' he informed her, his lips parting to show her that his front tooth was slightly crooked. 'My name's Pete—what's yours?'

'Louisa,' she told him, then bent her head, ending the conversation. 'If you'll excuse me, I have to get on with my work.'

She didn't want to be rude, but it was the simplest way. Pete got the message and left the shop—or so it seemed. When Louisa went for her lunch break he was waiting outside for her.

'Hi!' Pete's spiky head popped up beside her in the busy street. 'Fancy meeting you here?'

'Fancy,' she said drily, walking along the pavement away from him, the cars blaring their horns as they crawled along the wet road.

'Buy lunch for a starving musician?' he pleaded, turning the pockets of his faded blue jeans out. 'I'm stony broke. All I need is one little sandwich—I've been rehearsing all night.'

Louisa's cheeks dimpled at his sheer nerve. 'Go away,' she said, amused.

Pete followed her into the steamy little café around the corner, leaning against the counter as she ordered coffee and a sandwich for herself. His bright blue eyes ran over her with a smile.

'Tell you what,' he said, his bony hands raised in a compromise, 'I'll share your lunch—how's that?' and Louisa sighed, relenting and ordering him something to eat and drink.

The sound of china clattering all around them mingled noisily with the water that hissed steamily as it poured into coffee cups. They sat down at an oblong, plastic-topped table in the corner.

'What do you do?' she asked him as they ate. 'Apart from extort food from people?'

Pete grinned. 'A wandering minstrel I . . .' he intoned, unwrapping his sandwich from its plastic covering. 'This looks delightful,' he commented, eyeing the sandwich for a moment. Then he grinned again. 'I play rock music in clubs with some friends of mine—when my father isn't watching, that is.'

Louisa's brows rose. 'Daddy wouldn't approve?' she queried.

He put his sandwich down, uneaten. 'Afraid not. He says we're long-haired louts, and our music is a disgrace to the profession.' He shrugged. 'But who cares? We like it—and so do a lot of other people.'

She studied him, sipping her coffee, then asked, 'Are you successful?'

Pete looked at her out of the corner of his eye. 'A lot more successful at playing than I am at getting beautiful girls from bookshops to give me a date,' he hinted.

Her face tensed. She bent her head, ignoring his hint. She didn't want to get involved with anyone else—not after the disastrous way her relationship with Jacey had turned out.

Pete walked her back to the bookshop, stopping outside and delaying his goodbye for as long as possible. Louisa eventually had to tell him to go away.

'Why?' he asked when she said she didn't want to see him again. 'Because I'm a long-haired lout?' He grimaced, touching his hair. 'It's not that long—is it?'

It didn't even touch his collar, but it had nothing to do with it. 'No, but I just don't want to get involved,' Louisa said kindly, opening the shop door.

He watched her in silence, then shrugged. 'Okay. See you.' He wandered off in the other direction, scuffing his training shoes against the pavement as he walked.

Louisa didn't think she'd see him again. But the next day when she went for her lunch break, she noticed a long, brand new limousine pull up beside her.

'Hi.' Pete stepped out of the Rolls-Royce with a proud grin. 'Now it's my turn to take you to lunch,' he announced with more than a touch of self-satisfaction.

She allowed him to put her in the front seat, her eyes wide with incredulity. 'How many banks did you rob?' she asked, her voice breathless as they slid away smoothly.

'Just one,' he said lightly, 'and he'll kill me when he finds out.' He laughed as they pulled up outside an exclusive restaurant in Mayfair, lounging back in his seat. The jeans were gone, replaced by a well cut, expensive suit, and his hair was brushed back neatly.

Louisa looked at him slowly. 'Daddy's?' she asked.

Pete nodded, cutting out the engine. 'I forgot to mention—he owns about sixteen orchestras and a few opera houses around the world.'

Louisa stared at him in amazement.

By the end of the month, Peter Radcliffe was deeply in love with her. He bombarded her with flowers, presents, telephone calls. Her own feelings, however, were too deeply involved with Jacey for her to feel anything more than affection for him.

There was an innocence in Pete that touched something inside her. Her own childhood had been badly scarred by the stigma of illegitimacy, by poverty, and by the rough environment she had lived in. But Pete's family had shielded him from the realities of life.

Louisa still loved Jacey, though. He was a part of her, and she couldn't let go of his memory.

Pete took her to meet his father one evening. 'You'll know if he likes you,' he explained as they waited just inside the hall of the enormous white house. 'He'll try to rope you into listening to Wagner!'

Louisa frowned. Pete was taking her too seriously. 'I'm sure he'll just see me as another of your girl-friends,' she said gently.

Pete was about to speak, but a voice bellowed, 'Tell him I'm not in!'

Pete grimaced and whispered to her, 'That's my dear paternal relative. He should have been an opera star—he's always had a talent for yelling his guts out!'

Louisa gave him a little smile, but frowned as they heard more noises from along the hall.

'Infernal nuisance!' muttered an irritated voice, as a door opened. A man with a bald head and silver hair came out of the room wearing a dinner jacket and a very cross expression.

'Hi, Pop!' said Pete as the tall, elegant man

advanced towards him.

Mr Radcliffe eyed him with offended dignity. 'Kindly do not address me as Pop,' he said, his long Roman nose lifted in the air, his blue eyes beady.

Pete propelled Louisa forward. 'This is Louisa,' he told his father, and added, 'Be nice to her.'

Mr Radcliffe peered at her suspiciously. '*This* is Louisa?' he echoed, somewhat amazed. He studied her closely, then looked at his son with a smile. 'But she's normal! Good heavens, boy, why didn't you say so in the first place?'

Pete grinned. 'You'd never have believed me.'

Louisa watched the two men drily, feeling as though she were a tennis ball being passed from one to the other. 'Do you mind?' she said with a warm smile. 'I am still here, you know.'

Mr Radcliffe smiled. 'Beg your pardon, my dear, but my son has a habit of bringing the strangest creatures home. When he was a teenager, he used to bring the most unspeakable objects home and masquerade them as females.'

Louisa could believe that. Pete was only just kicking the habit of rebelling against everything his father stood for, and he was nearly twenty-seven years old. It was really time he stopped it.

'I say,' Mr Radcliffe stroked his jaw contemplatively, 'do you remember that creature with the fluorescent green hair? Green!' He shuddered, looking at Louisa. 'Punk rocker, you know,' he informed her gravely, 'in my own home! Never thought I'd live to see the day.'

Louisa's eyes danced. 'Well,' she said, laughing, 'I'm not a punk rocker, I'm afraid. Sorry if I've disappointed you.'

'Good lord, no!' Mr Radcliffe laughed, his expression jovial. 'You're a pretty little thing—wouldn't do to see you with safety-pins in your nose.' He took her arm with a smile. 'Won't you take a drink with me, my dear?' he invited, leading her towards the room he had emerged from.

Pete followed, grinning at Louisa while she did her best to ignore him, giving all her attention to his father.

'Do you like Verdi, my dear?' Mr Radcliffe asked hopefully.

'He liked you!' Pete told her with pride as he drove her home.

The evening had definitely been a success. Peter's father had cornered her attention, making sure she had everything she could possibly want, taking the utmost trouble to see that her glass was always filled. She had been flattered and pleased. She had felt a deeper affection towards Pete as he grinned triumphantly across at her.

'I liked him too,' she said, smiling as night-time London flashed by in a glowing blur.

'My mother would have liked you,' Pete murmured, his eyes distant.

Louisa put her hand over his, silently comforting. She knew only too well what it was like to be without one of your parents. She had often felt as though a part of her was missing, a part of her identity had been lost, thrown away by a careless stranger.

Tonight, she had felt she had *belonged*, truly belonged. Not the way she felt with Jacey, because their love was deep and intense, real and compelling. But with Pete and his father she had somehow felt ... as though she were part of a family, a warm family unit.

'Tell you what,' said Pete as they pulled up outside her flat, 'I'll take you to the opera in the spring. That'll be right up your street—all those huge people bellowing their insides out all over the place!'

She laughed, her cheeks dimpling. 'Sounds like fun,' she agreed, tongue in cheek.

'Of course,' Pete switched off the engine, leaning towards her, 'you'd have to marry me first.'

Louisa stiffened, her body going icy cold. She didn't know how to reply, didn't know how to look at him. Marriage to Pete would be like marriage to the brother she had never had.

Louisa reached for the doorhandle. 'I have to go.' She stepped out on to the pavement and looked back at him coolly. 'See you tomorrow night.'

Pete looked hurt, his face vulnerable, his eyes sad. 'Okay,' he said quietly. 'See you.' He started the engine and drove off into the night, red tail lights softening in the distance.

Louisa looked up at her flat. *Where are you, Jacey?* she thought, her heart hurting, her eyes glossing over with a sheen of private agony. Will I ever see you again? She stood in the chill, empty night for a long moment, then went slowly into her flat.

The flat was chillingly silent. The emptiness ate into her heart, making her eyes close tightly, willing the pain away. She was alone and she desperately needed Jacey.

How many times, she thought, have I needed him and known he won't be there? She had lost count of the days, the weeks, the hours. It wasn't a surrogate father she was looking for—it was a man who cared for her, someone who she knew would always be there.

Her own father had deserted her before she was even born. Her stepfather had never taken the slightest bit of interest in her. Now when she finally thought she had found the man to take care of her, even he had walked out on her.

You bastard, Jacey, she thought, and a hot tear squeezed out from under her lid. Wiping it away with one hand like a vulnerable child, she caught sight of herself in the mirror.

Defeated. She looked as though she'd been pushed into a corner and beaten over the head until she slumped, defeated and broken. He's broken me, she thought bitterly. She didn't even have the energy to scream out like a wounded animal, to shout and break things at the injustice of it.

It was then that she decided. Forget him, she told herself angrily. He's forgotten you. The reason he could still hurt her was because she had never let go of him, never let him fade into her past. The past could only hurt her if she let it stay in the present.

Filled with a new courage and determination, she turned away from the broken woman in the mirror, knowing that she did not want to be that woman, refused to be that woman.

She went into the bathroom and stripped her clothes off, stepping into the cool enamel bath and switching the shower on. The needles of water woke her up, kept her mind alive, made her feel cold inside as she thought of Jacey.

A sound from the door made her stiffen, and she turned, eyes flying open in shock.

'Jacey!' Her voice strangled her, her naked body froze.

'Good evening,' he drawled, and the predatory green eyes ran lazily over her, lingering on the warm, wet swell of her breasts, noting the swift hardening of her nipples. 'Don't let me stop you. You were touching yourself so lovingly—who were you thinking of?'

She felt hot all over, her face burning, her heart hammering crazily. 'I wasn't,' she said through a tight throat.

One dark brow rose. 'No?'

She shook her head jerkily, her eyes a wild, startled black. 'When did you get back?' Her chest was hurting so badly she could barely speak. 'How did you get in?' She tried to breathe normally, but she could hear herself dragging air into her lungs as though she was dying.

'Your landlord let me in,' he told her, eyes narrowing harshly as he added, 'Four hours ago.'

An intense silence followed and Louisa slowly remembered that she was naked, at once sliding her hands to cover herself, her face burning, turning her head away.

'Would you,' she asked huskily, 'would you pass me that towel?' One pale hand outstretched as she pointed to the pale blue bathtowel on the rack beside him.

He slowly reached out one sinewy hand, sliding the towel off the rack and holding it out of her reach. 'Here,' he said softly, tilting his head in sardonic challenge, 'come and get it.'

Louisa flushed, unable to move for a moment. Then she stepped out of the bath, her legs unsteady, and walked towards him, conscious of the way his eyes almost devoured her body as she did so.

Jacey held the towel away from her. 'So shy, my darling?' he drawled as she tried to grab for it unsteadily, almost losing her balance.

She tried to stop trembling. 'Please,' she said in a pained husky voice.

The hard mouth firmed. 'Forgotten me so soon?' he asked in a tight drawl. 'Or has your wealthy friend given you ideas above your station?'

She froze. Then she moistened her lips, pretending innocence. 'Wealthy friend?'

His eyes narrowed. 'Your memory is faulty,' he said smokily. 'He drove you home in a very expensive car. Very sleek, very powerful. Is that what turns you on?' The dark brows rose. 'Power?'

Louisa felt the scarlet heat rush to her face. 'How long have you been here?' she asked, half angry, half frightened.

'Long enough.' His voice was harder now, and she knew he was angry. She caught her breath as she felt his long hard fingers trail across her neck with sensual deliberation. 'Why didn't he come in? Too tired? Or had he already taken you to bed at his place?'

The biting angry voice made her push his hand angrily from her neck. 'Don't touch me!' she burst out, shaking, eyes wild.

Jacey's eyes leapt with violent flames. 'Don't touch you?' he echoed tightly. 'Why? Am I so distasteful to you now? Has he turned you against your own kind? Do you only sleep with rich fools?'

She stared at him, bitterly angry. 'It isn't like that!'

'No?' he said, his mouth biting out the words. 'You tell me what it is like.'

'He's a friend, nothing more.' Louisa was breathing hard, her breasts rising and falling, her heart hurting as it hammered against her chest, her pulses drumming.

His gaze swept over her naked body. 'Is he a good lover?' he asked through his teeth, and Louisa jerked back in shock, feeling the anger boil up inside her.

'Goodnight, Jacey,' she said through barely parted lips, and started to walk past him with as much dignity as she could.

Something inside him snapped. 'Don't walk away from me, you little bitch!' he bit out, pulling her violently back until she landed hard against him, her damp skin trembling against him, her thighs pressing against his.

They stared at each other intently, breathing hard. Louisa felt as though someone had touched a burning flame to her as his fingers burnt into her shoulders.

'How long has it been going on?' Jacey asked under his breath.

'A month,' she said breathlessly. 'I was lonely, and I needed a friend. What did you expect me to do?'

His jaw clamped tightly. 'I asked you to wait for me.'

Tears of rage and frustration stung her eyes. 'You asked too much!' she snapped, her throat tight. 'I didn't think you were coming back. If I'd known, I would have . . .'

'What?' he cut in. 'Hidden your lover under the bed? Pretended everything was still the same?' He shook his black head, his breathing unsteady. 'I wouldn't stand for that, Louisa—you know that.'

He was right and she knew it. But she would never have got involved with Pete if she'd expected Jacey to come back. Now she was caught in a painful triangle of her own making.

'I know,' she whispered, her body straining towards him with a hunger which she was unaware showed as clearly as though it blazed out of her, 'but I can't trust you any more, Jacey. How can we go on if there's no trust?'

His eyes burnt into her soul. 'How can we stop if we feel like this?' he countered, his voice thickening.

She caught her breath, and his black head swooped until his hard mouth moved hungrily over hers, draining her, sending her heart racing, her hands clutching in his hair, clinging to him heatedly.

He drew away roughly, his face flushed. 'Tell him,' he said thickly. 'Tell him tomorrow. I want him right out of the picture.'

Louisa nodded, swaying against him as though drugged. 'Yes.'

His eyes closed for a moment, then he pushed away from her, going to the door of the flat. Louisa stared at his back incredulously, then ran after him.

'Jacey!' she called breathlessly. 'Are you . . .' she swallowed, her eyes intense as she watched him. 'Are you coming back?'

He inclined his head. 'Tomorrow.' The door closed behind him and Louisa stared at it in angry disbelief as she heard his heels click on the stairs.

I'm a fool, she thought bitterly as she made her way to the restaurant to meet Pete. Jacey offers me nothing but lies and secrets—what will he give me except the same agony he's put me through ever since we met?

She sighed, clinging to the rail of the platform of the bus. She would have to think of something to tell Pete. She couldn't tell him about Jacey because it would hurt him too much. Better to tell him she had just changed her mind.

The bus chugged away as she stepped off it at the last moment, and her mind was confused as she saw the restaurant looming up ahead. She made her way towards it with a blank expression.

Pete was waiting for her. 'Hi!' he said, kissing her as she walked in. 'You're late. You're worse than our drummer—he's always late too.'

'Sorry,' Louisa said with a smile as they made their way to the table through the crowded noisy restaurant. 'I missed the bus and had to wait ages for another one.'

Pete pulled his tie, undoing the top button as he always did. He hated ties. 'You and your buses,' he said, sitting opposite her. 'Why don't you learn to drive—get a car?'

She raised her brows. 'Because I can't afford one.' She flicked the napkin open on her lap. Then she noticed the waiter pouring champagne in their glasses and became uneasy. 'Champagne?' she queried.

Pete looked excited, a restless gleam in his eyes.

'Special occasion,' he said, grinning. 'You won't have to bother with buses anymore.'

She sat very still, watching him worriedly. 'What do you mean?'

He raised his champagne in a toast. 'To dear old Daddy,' he said, smiling at her, 'who gave me a big fat cheque this morning and told me to spare no expense.'

Louisa's heart stopped beating as he reached into his jacket pocket and produced a blue box which he opened. The glitter of diamonds and sapphires flashed under the light, the white-gold band nestling against blue velvet.

'If you're lucky,' said Pete in a casual voice, extending the ring to her with a bony hand, 'I might agree to marry you.'

Louisa stared at the ring for a full moment, unable to speak. Despite his casual approach, she saw the intensity in his eyes as he watched her. 'Peter, I'm not in love with you,' she said slowly, and raised her eyes to his face. 'You know that.'

There was a little silence, and she saw the light go out of his eyes. Then he gave an uncertain laugh. 'I always know someone's cross with me when they call me Peter,' he said, taking the ring out of the box and slipping it on Louisa's finger. 'Only my father calls me Peter.'

She bit her lip anxiously. 'Did you hear what I said?'

He was totally still for a moment, then he reddened, looking away. 'Don't say no, Louisa,' he said huskily. 'Think it over before you give me a definite answer.'

She stayed silent. The ring was frighteningly comfortable on her hand. The truth was—she was tempted, sorely tempted. Jacey's painful mixture of intense love and secrecy would destroy her in the end. Pete was offering her security, contentment.

Pete could give her a name. After so long without the cloak of respectability, the surname of her father, Pete would be able to give her his name. Could Jacey do that?

I don't even *know* Jacey's surname, she thought with sudden bitterness. All I know about him is that his name's Jacey, he lives in a flat near here, and he works in a dead-end job. And how could he love her, when he hid behind lies and secrets, never letting his true identity shine through?

Slowly she reached out and touched the ring on her left hand. 'I don't know,' she murmured, 'I just don't know.'

Pete watched her intensely, his face strikingly vulnerable, the hollow cheekbones tight with tension. 'Just wear it for the moment,' he said, the tension evident in his voice. 'No strings—no promises.'

The chips were down. Either she gambled everything on Jacey or she settled for security and contentment. But how can you gamble on a mystery? How can you gamble on something that doesn't really exist? After all, what was Jacey? Nothing but a magnetic shadow, a powerfully drawn silhouette with raw character—but none of the details drawn in.

'Okay, Pete,' Louisa said quietly, raising her eyes to his, her expression thoughtful, 'just for the moment. But remember what you said, and don't try to pull any strings.'

Her mind was confused as he drove her home.

Jacey hadn't been in touch with her all day. For all she knew he had gone away again, and the thought made her heart hurt, her head pushing forward reasons for anger.

But Jacey was waiting for her.

She didn't notice him until the very last moment. Then she saw him out of the corner of her eye as she walked up the path to her flat.

'You're late,' he said coolly, walking towards her, his black hair gleaming under the bright orange glow of the street light. 'I've been here since ten.'

Louisa felt her nerves begin to jangle. She slipped her left hand behind her back to hide the ring. 'You didn't get in touch with me today,' she said, feeling her pulses thud. 'Where were you?'

Jacey shrugged lazily. 'Biding my time,' he drawled. He looked intensely sexy in dark jeans and a black tight-fitting sweater, his powerful chest outlined, his slim waist and lean hips devastatingly attractive.

She nodded, her hands trembling as she slipped her key in the door. He would be violently angry when he knew she hadn't finished with Pete. She went into the empty communal hall, and he followed her up to the flat.

He closed the door of the living room after them, leaning against it lazily, watching her. 'Did you tell him?'

She felt her heart begin to thud faster with nerves. Putting her bag down on an armchair, she slipped off the light cardigan in silence, unable to lie to him.

The green eyes narrowed speculatively. 'I asked you a question,' he said under his breath.

Louisa swallowed. Her wide, frightened eyes told him the answer, and he came towards her, his face tight. His hands gripped her shoulders in an iron grip.

'Damn you!' he muttered tightly. 'Did you tell him or not?'

Louisa looked away, her face hot. 'No,' she said huskily.

The lean fingers bit into her flesh, making her wince. 'Why not?' he asked tightly, and she looked up, seeing the harsh angular face harden with anger.

'I couldn't,' she said shakily, frightened because she could see how angry he was, and it made her pulse leap furiously with fear and excitement. 'I didn't know what to say.'

Jacey gave a harsh crack of laughter. 'You mean you'd rather keep him hanging around in case I go away again.' He surveyed her face with leaping eyes. 'Is that closer to the truth? Or do you just like the idea of three in the bed?'

The insult took her breath away. 'You selfish bastard!' she breathed, her eyes wide with incredulity that he could be so cruel. 'You have no right to demand explanations. You went away and left me—now you expect me to jump every time you bark!'

'Bite,' he corrected through his teeth. Then his eye caught the flash of diamonds on her hand, and his hand shot out, gripping hers, lifting it up and staring at it. 'What the hell is this?' he asked under his breath.

Louisa swallowed, her throat dry and tight. 'He asked me to marry him,' she managed to say, her heart hammering with such force that it made her chest hurt.

There was a silence so intense that Louisa's face burnt, her hands shaking as she stood against Jacey, watching the hard-boned face tense with control as he looked at her ring.

After a long moment, he asked slowly, 'Are you going to?' and his voice was deep, controlled.

Louisa wanted to hit back at him, hurt him as badly as he had hurt her. 'Yes,' she said below her breath, and had the satisfaction of seeing him tense, his body stiffening as though from a physical blow while she watched defiantly.

His face was rigid, stony. 'You love him?' His voice was taut.

Her throat constricted painfully. 'Yes.' she lied, 'I love him.'

The silence that followed was charged with emotion, an electricity that came from both her and Jacey as they faced each other, his hand biting into her.

'I see,' he said tightly, his voice thick with anger. 'Why didn't you tell me last night? It would have saved us both a lot of trouble.' His mouth twisted in a cruel smile. 'Or were you waiting for the fish to bite? Hadn't he asked you? Did you want to be sure before you burnt your bridges?' his voice sniped at her bitingly.

She almost flinched from the leaping violence in his eyes. 'You were angry last night,' she said, her voice husky with fear and excitement, 'I wanted to wait until you cooled down.'

He smiled, and her blood ran cold. 'You got the wrong man, lady,' he muttered between his teeth. 'Last night was child's play.' He studied her, his eyes hard and dangerous. 'Is it his money? Is that what you're after?'

She shrugged. 'If that's what you prefer to believe.'

Jacey's eyes flashed with a warning of danger. 'Don't play games with me, Louisa,' he grated. 'If his money turns you on I want to know about it.'

She jerked away from him, frightened by the insistent, angry questions. 'It's none of your business any more, Jacey!' she said angrily, rubbing her upper arms, feeling the tenderness of her skin where he had hurt her. 'You threw me away—now you'll have to live with it.'

His teeth snapped together like a steel trap. 'You mercenary little bitch!' he said bitingly, his hands clenching at his sides. 'That's a lie and you know it. You just want to marry money.'

Louisa stared at him, her eyes flashing an angry black. 'Why not?' she said bitterly. He blamed her at every turn. 'He can give me everything I need.'

Jacey's eyes blazed with violent emotion. 'And I can't?'

She laughed, her throat tight, her eyes stinging with angry tears. 'What can you give me? Yourself? For how long?' She laughed again, shaking her head. 'Two or three years at the most, then you'd disappear into nowhere and I'd never see you again.' She drew a ragged breath, her face tight and pale. 'Well, it's not good enough, Jacey.'

He watched her, his face working with anger and emotion. His hands clenched and unclenched at his sides as he controlled his violent temper. The silence was filled with the sounds of their racing heartbeats, their ragged angry breathing.

'Thank God I found out in time,' he said bitingly. 'Any man who marries you might just as well take poison or slit his throat.' His eyes raked her from head to foot with contempt. 'Marry him, and I hope your lonely bed makes you very happy. He'll have you climbing the walls with frustration in minutes.'

She raised her head, her eyes bitter. 'Silk-clad walls, Jacey. Something you could never give me.'

He drew a terse breath. 'You bitch!' he muttered contemptuously, and slammed out of the flat without another word.

Louisa listened in silence as his harsh footsteps echoed in the dark street outside. Then her hands went to her face, tears of rage and pain falling over her cheeks as she stumbled to a chair and collapsed in it, crying wrenching sobs.

CHAPTER THREE

FATE was laughing at her.

After months of living in dreamland, the bubble had finally burst. And Louisa had hit the ground with a resounding crash, flung into an icy, hostile world.

Life was like that. One moment you're up, the next moment you're down; flat on your back wondering what on earth happened. It just goes to show, she thought dazedly, you should never laugh at fate, never laugh at tomorrow—one day tomorrow will turn right around and laugh at you.

For a moment the tormented black eyes flashed with anger. Jacey had had no right to treat her that way. Their arguments had been unnecessary, he should have been able to confide in her. Instead he had turned his back on her when she needed him most.

She sighed bitterly. Fate had only ever been kind to her twice in her life, and even then it had played a bizarre joke on her by sending both gifts at the same time. Pete's appearance had simply come at the wrong time.

She loved Jacey totally—it was an intense attraction, combined with a deep knowledge that he belonged to her, was a part of her. But she felt a good deal of affection for Pete.

She felt protective towards him. He had an infectious smile, a happy-go-lucky attitude to life brought about by his naïvety about the realities of the world.

She turned more and more towards Pete as the pain inside her grew. The more she needed Jacey, the more she clung to Pete. He was all she had left, and she just didn't feel strong enough to make it on her own any more.

'Does he know about Jacey?' Scotty asked her one afternoon while they took their coffee break in the shop.

'No.' Louisa sipped the steaming coffee, refusing to meet Mr Scott's eyes.

Scotty sighed heavily. 'Ah, it's a bad thing you're doing to him, lassie,' he said deeply, and the watery blue eyes were filled with concern. 'He has a right to know.'

Louisa's lips firmed as she bent her head, studying the counter blankly. Pete did have a right to know, but she didn't know what the point in telling him was. It would only hurt him.

Scotty watched her, then shrugged his wiry shoulders, grimacing. 'Have it your own way,' he said, and added worriedly, 'But I don't like it. I don't like it at all.'

'It would only hurt him,' Louisa pointed out irritably.

Scotty shook his grey head. 'I meant Jacey,' he said quietly. 'He's a complete mystery to me, but there's one thing I do know—he's not the type to take this lying down.'

She frowned, her eyes narrowing warily. 'What do you mean?'

Scotty's grey brows rose. 'I mean that he's the type who likes to get revenge.' He shrugged. 'Seen it in his eyes. Strange eyes,' he murmured, looking worriedly at the wall, 'like a wolf . . . that's what he reminds me of—a wolf. And he'll come back with his teeth bared.'

Louisa stared at him. Prophetic words? she thought, shuddering with half fear, half excitement. The thought of Jacey coming back for revenge made her heart hammer furiously at her chest.

'Congratulations, my dear!' Mr Radcliffe was pumping her hand, his round face beaming with smiles, the hollowed eyes alive, crinkling at the edges as he looked at her.

'Thank you,' she replied with a blank smile. The party was giving her a headache. It was split into two factions—one half dressed as though they were meeting the Queen, the other half dressed as though they were at a rock concert.

She looked down at the ring on her left hand. Now it was official. She was engaged to Peter Radcliffe, and their forthcoming wedding had been announced in *The Times* by Mr Radcliffe.

Louisa suddenly felt very empty. I'm a silly fool, she thought sadly. I've thrown away Jacey, who was worth more than anything else in the world to me, for the sake of winning a petty argument.

'Looking forward to July?' Pete popped up beside her, his spiky blond hair ruffled, his face flushed as he downed another drink.

'Of course,' she replied with a tight smile. Only three weeks to their wedding. Only three months since Jacey had left her. It seemed like a lifetime to her.

Pete gazed around the room at the conflicting groups of guests and laughed. 'Doesn't it look weird? Who knows what it'll look like at the wedding. The priest'll think someone's playing a joke on him!'

Louisa smiled blankly and looked away. She wanted to go home, she was sick of this party. It made her feel so guilty.

Mr Radcliffe peered at his son. 'I hope all this means a change for the better, my boy. Wouldn't want to think of Louisa hobnobbing with your long-haired friends.'

Louisa laughed at the irritation on Peter's face and touched his arm gently. 'He's got a point,' she said softly. 'Which world are we going to live in?' The words made her feel even more guilty, because she knew no world was complete for her without Jacey.

Pete frowned thoughtfully. 'I don't know.' He laughed ruefully. 'Most of the time I don't even know which world is reality. They're both real. It's like seeing both sides of life and having to adjust each time you move into the other side.'

Louisa smiled her understanding quietly. He was torn between a life he had built for himself and the life his parents had given him. Poor Peter! She knew how he felt.

Turning away, she went out into the hall for a moment's respite. Pete frowned for a moment, then followed her.

'What's up?' he asked, studying her bent head, the light picking out strands of midnight-blue in her hair.

She raised her head, her eyes honest. 'I want to go home.'

His face smoothed over expressionlessly. 'All right,' he said with control, 'I'll drive you.'

She laid a hand on his arm, knowing that the

time had come for her to be totally honest with him. It would do no good for her to pretend feelings that didn't exist. It would only hurt him more in the long run.

'Alone,' she said quietly, 'I want to go home alone. I don't know,' she shrugged, sighing, 'I just need time to think.'

He froze into silence, studying her. He was hurt, she could see that, but it couldn't be helped. He nodded jerkily. 'I'll get you a car.'

Louisa stepped outside the front door into the cool night air. She couldn't face going back into the party, even to say goodbye to them all. She needed to be alone for a while.

A long black limousine slid towards her like a panther and she looked up. A man in black uniform got out and said softly, 'Your car, Miss Faulkner.'

She nodded, and turned her head, wondering if she should wait for Pete. But he was probably too upset to even speak to her. She slid into the back of the car, and it pulled away smoothly while Louisa shut her eyes and relaxed.

When she opened her eyes, she frowned, looking out of the window. Then she leaned forward and tapped on the glass partition.

'We're going the wrong way,' she told the chauffeur. 'My flat is in Belgrave Road.'

There was a short silence. 'We're not going the wrong way.'

Louisa sat very still, her heart thudding. 'I think we are,' she said uneasily.

The man's eyes lifted to hers in the rear-view mirror. The four doors thumped shut, locking her in, and her eyes darted like a trapped animal's as she looked around. There was very little she could do. She sat back tensely, waiting to see where they were going. She wanted to scream, but there seemed no point.

The car eventually turned into a private driveway, crawling along the gravel road until they stopped at the house. Louisa looked out, her eyes tracing the white columns, the coach light over the front door gleaming yellow in the darkness.

The chauffeur opened her door. 'This way, please,' he said quietly.

Louisa stepped back as he closed the car door behind her. 'Where are we?' she asked, her eyes narrowed.

The chauffeur smiled. 'Never mind that now, miss,' he said softly, and led her into the house, along the exquisitely furnished hall to the room at the end of it. 'If you'd wait in here, miss,' he said politely, closing the door behind her.

Her heart beating with nervousness, Louisa stood in the centre of the room. It was beautifully decorated—by someone who obviously had a lot of money to spare. She looked around, her eyes curious.

The door opened behind her, and she spun, eyes widening.

'Jacey?' she whispered, incredulously.

He leaned against the door, his broad shoulders encased in a superbly cut black dinner jacket, his waist and lean hips emphasised by a smooth, tight-fitting black waistcoat, his long legs making her knees go weak.

'Jacey?' he queried softly, then shook his black head. 'Jacey's dead. He doesn't exist any more.'

She took one slow step towards him, her eyes

narrowed, amazed. 'I don't understand . . .' she said slowly, staring at him.

'No,' he drawled, his hard mouth indenting sardonically, 'I don't suppose you do.'

She stared at him for a long moment in stunned silence. Then she demanded, 'Why are you here, in this house?' She frowned, her head tilting. 'Are they friends of yours?'

He shook his head. 'The house is mine.'

Her mouth parted with amazement. Her eyes ran over the expensive décor of the room once more, taking in the antiques, the original paintings that hung on the walls. This room alone was worth hundreds of thousands of pounds.

'But . . .' she began haltingly, shaking her head, 'but where did you get the money from?'

The firm mouth crooked cynically. 'Questions,' he drawled lazily, studying her, 'always questions. Do you never take anything on face value?' One brow rose in barbed amusement. 'Except money, of course.'

Louisa flushed angrily. 'That isn't fair, Jacey. . . .' she began.

His voice sliced through like a whiplash. 'Not Jacey!' he said bitingly, then he watched her for a moment in an intense silence before shrugging lazily and saying, 'I told you—Jacey doesn't exist any more. He never really did.'

Louisa felt her pulses leap furiously with fear. The hard-boned face had changed over the months. Ruthlessness was now stamped on his angular face, power was ingrained in the menacing glitter of his eyes.

'Then,' she said shakily, 'if you're not Jacey, who are you?'

He studied her through thick black lashes that rested on his hard tanned cheek. Then he pushed away from the door, walking lazily over towards her.

'My name is Jason Knight,' he told her coolly, and she started to back away from him, frightened by the sinister look in his green eyes. 'You see?' he drawled, stopping a few feet from her. 'You barely know me any more, or you wouldn't be frightened of me.'

Louisa lifted her head, her face defiant. 'I'm not frightened of you,' she lied, controlling the leaping pulse at the hollow of her white throat.

'No?' One dark brow rose, his face hardening as his gaze travelled over her. 'You should be.'

Her throat tightened. He was a stranger—a menacing stranger who threatened her with every look of those predatory eyes, every flick of his black lashes.

She looked away from his piercing stare. 'Why have you brought me here?' she asked in a low voice.

Jacey slid one long finger into the pocket of his black waistcoat. 'You wanted to marry money,' he said in a cold voice, and a smile touched his lips. 'Here it is.'

She stared at him bitterly, her lips tightening into a firm line. Her face whitened, the huge black eyes flashing, intent on his face as she watched him.

'You really believe that, don't you?' she said in a low angry voice. 'You really think I'm out for money.'

'Yes,' he said tightly, and the long fingers clenched at his side. 'You were ambitious when I met you, and you haven't changed much. You've just got more ambition instead of less.'

'That's a lie!' she burst out, her lips trembling with indignation. 'I may have wanted a better life, but that's only because I'd had a rough deal . . .'

'And I haven't?' he cut in bitingly.

A silence fell, and they both stared at each other intently, electricity crackling tangibly between them. Then Jacey relaxed, his body less tense than before.

'You have the night to think it over,' he said in a cool voice, his words clipped. 'When you've decided, we'll set the wheels in motion.'

He walked towards the door, and Louisa followed him. 'Decided what?' she asked quickly, catching hold of the dark expensive material of his jacket sleeve.

His eyes slowly dropped to her hand. Then he looked at her, his eyes hard and unreadable. Louisa could hear her heart hammering wildly against her breastbone.

'Whether you'd rather marry Peter Radcliffe's money,' he said in a dark hostile voice, 'or mine.'

Her eyes widened as she heard him speak. 'How do you know his name? How did you know where he lived?' she asked in a shaky whisper.

Jacey's mouth crooked cynically. 'My men are very loyal,' he drawled, 'they do as they're told. I only have to lift a finger to get all the information I want.'

She was bewildered, out of her depth. This hostile stranger who stood before her frightened her. The intense emotion no longer blazed in his eyes, the sensual curve of his mouth had hardened under the weight of cynicism.

'I want my answer in the morning,' Jacey said coldly, opening the door and stepping into the hall. He looked along the hall and crooked one long finger. 'Mitchell,' he said crisply, and the chauffeur came forward, 'drive the young lady home, and make sure she stays there—alone.'

He left the hall, going into another room, and Louisa followed the chauffeur to the limousine, her mind whirling with confusion, her heart pounding with total disorder.

Jacey haunted her all night. He frightened her. The intensity of their feelings for each other was now boiling just beneath the surface, and she sensed an ultimate explosion if she didn't watch her step.

Giving her one night to decide was so unfair. Yet if she really loved him, surely the choice would be easy? She sighed, twisting and turning in her bed, staring into the lonely darkness. How could she make a choice which would send her rocketing into heaven and hell? Their relationship had kept her there always, just between heaven and hell, and she wasn't sure if she could take it for life. Heaven was so good, but hell was so violently painful. And that was what he was offering her. If she married Pete she would have security, a name, a family, a home—and probably boredom. That was one thing that could never be said of Jacey. He had always kept her charged up like an overheated engine.

She looked around and saw the alternatives life was offering her. She could leave both of them, start again—a new dawn, as Jacey had once said. But that would be as cold and lonely as her life before Jacey, and she knew she wouldn't be able to do it.

She could marry Pete and be secure but restless. Or she could marry Jacey and plunge herself on a possible path to destruction. But life without him had been so miserable, so painful.

Her mind was so confused that all she could do was writhe in torment until dawn broke, and sleep claimed her, still undecided, still lost in confusion.

The bell woke her. She blinked, her eyes heavy, then sat up, her heart thudding fast. Jumping out of bed, she slipped her wrap on and ran downstairs to answer the door.

Jacey stood outside, looking dangerously sexy in a dark suit, the waistcoat tight on his lean hard stomach, his shirt open at the neck to expose his brown throat. Louisa felt her mouth go dry with longing.

She shivered, suddenly shy in front of him. Pulling her robe together, she said, 'I haven't made up my mind.' She felt herself tremble with nerves. 'I need more time.'

His face tightened. 'Too bad,' he said harshly, towering over her with a distinct air of menace. 'You don't have time. Either decide now or we forget the whole thing.'

Louisa's frown was pained. 'Please,' she said softly, eyes pleading.

Jacey gave a harsh impatient sigh. 'I'll wait in the car,' he muttered, and turned on his heel. He shot a look at her over his shoulder as he walked. 'Be down in ten minutes.'

Louisa closed the door and climbed the stairs to her flat with a heavy heart. The triangle had closed in on her suddenly, and she had no idea how to fight her way out of it. The change in Jacey was almost beyond belief.

She dressed quickly in tight jeans and a white blouse, brushing her hair quickly and applying eyeliner, mascara and lipstick before going downstairs.

She hesitated, her body tense, then opened the front door and went into the street.

The car door swung open, the engine purring like a thoroughbred cat; sleek, black, its coat glistening in the early morning sunlight. She slid in beside Jacey in the front seat.

The car shot away smoothly, and she slid a tentative glance at him. His face was outlined harshly against the blue-grey sky, the line of cheek and jaw assertive, freshly shaven. Louisa bit her lip and looked away, and they drove on in silence.

As they turned into the driveway of his house a while later, Louisa looked up apprehensively. The great white stone walls seemed to loom as though it was a prison. She had no wish to become a bird in a gilded cage.

They were silent as they walked to the house, their heels crunching on the gravel path, the tiny stones damp, the early morning chorus of birds welcoming them.

Jacey closed the study door behind him with a click that made her whole body tense in alarm.

They faced each other across the silence, their eyes locked together in a battle for supremacy.

'Well?' the question was clipped from his mouth.

Moistening her lips, Louisa forced control into her voice as she said, 'I need more time. I can't give you my answer yet.'

'You can,' he said coolly, his dark face unreadable, 'and you will.'

Louisa drew a deep breath. He had no right to force her into this position. She didn't want to marry this hostile man; she wanted to marry the Jacey she had met and fallen in love with so long ago.

'You can't force me,' she told him in a tense voice, raising her head with a mixture of self-defence and attack. No one had ever affected her like this before. No man, woman or child. Jacey had burst into her life and crashed through her defences leaving her indecisive, weak and confused. She had once been so strong. Now she felt like a fool, and she didn't like that feeling one little bit.

His mouth indented sardonically. 'Can't I?' he drawled.

Her face tightened angrily. 'I can't make a snap decision. There's too much to take into account for that.' It was the rest of her life that was being decided, and that meant a lot to her.

Jacey came closer and she found herself backing nervously. 'Your back is against the wall, Louisa,' he said tightly. 'You're marrying Radcliffe in three weeks. Do you think he'll thank you for jilting him at the altar? Wouldn't he prefer some advance warning?'

She swallowed, shutting her eyes to the words. She didn't want to hurt Peter—she owed him more than that. But if she went ahead with the marriage, wouldn't she be hurting him more than ever? Hurting myself, too, she thought bitterly.

'Don't you think I know that?' she said in a low painful voice. 'Do you think I want to hurt him?'

Jacey gave a harsh crack of laughter. 'Why not?' he said bitingly. 'You hurt me.'

Her heart hurt, and she raised her head jerkily

to look at him, feeling her pulses drum crazily at her throat and temples.

'I didn't mean to hurt you, Jacey,' she said softly, frowning.

His jaw clamped. 'Don't give it a thought,' he said tightly. 'It was too long ago.' He thrust his hands into the pockets of the superbly cut black trousers, and she watched him, biting her lip, wishing there was something she could say to eradicate everything that had happened in the past.

But it was hopeless. Rage had made her say things she had made herself believe were true. Circumstances, she thought with a bitter smile, circumstances made me react that way.

'Besides,' Jacey was watching her, seeing the gamut of emotions on her face, 'you won't be marrying Jacey. You'll be Mrs Jason Knight.'

She gave a hollow laugh. 'Where's the difference? You can change your name, change your surroundings—but you can never change who you are inside.' Her eyes held his intensely. 'No one can ever do that.'

His mouth crooked cynically. 'That's where you're wrong,' he said, his voice sardonic, laced with bitterness. 'Jacey was naïve. He fell for a mercenary bitch.' He took a step towards her, his face hardening. 'That's what you are, my darling—a mercenary, greedy little bitch.'

Her lips were tight. 'How kind!' she snapped, eyes flashing.

He smiled, making her blood run cold. 'Don't mention it,' he drawled, and her fists clenched uselessly at her sides. 'So,' Jacey tilted his black head to one side, raising one dark brow in enquiry, 'what's it to be? My money? Or Radcliffe's?'

Her heart was thudding a deadly rhythm, her eyes pained. 'I think I preferred you as you were,' she said in a low voice.

His eyes blazed with an emotion which she found alarming. 'Too bad,' he snapped. 'You forced me back into this way of life, now you're going to have to live with it.'

Louisa stared at him for a long moment, her pulses throbbing with anger. 'That's where you're wrong,' she said angrily, 'because my answer is no.'

He stared at her, his body rigid. Louisa watched as rage fought emotion on his dark face, feelings she couldn't comprehend raging in his brilliant green eyes.

Then she moved. Jacey followed. They both ran for the door at the same time, and he reached her just as her hand touched the handle.

'Not so fast,' he muttered between his teeth. His fingers bit into her wrist. 'I want your reasons before you leave.'

She turned angry eyes on him, her face taut. 'Why the hell do you think?' she snapped.

He looked at her for a long intense moment. 'Love?' he clipped out eventually, the word forced between his white teeth.

More lies? Louisa asked herself bitterly, and was suddenly sick of the whole charade. Fight pain with pain and it doubles back on you, she realised wearily.

'No,' she said on a heavy sigh, raising her eyes to his, giving in at last to the need for him which had been fighting her common sense. 'No, I don't love him any more than I'd love a friend.'

He considered her in silence for a second. 'Then you'll marry me?' he asked tautly.

She nodded, bending her head in defeat. Fighting him was draining. There were two men in her life, and she knew damned well which one of them she loved. Jacey was hers; she had known it from the beginning and she knew it now. There was no point in any more lies.

'Good.' His voice was crisp, businesslike. 'Break it off with Radcliffe, wind up your flat and your job as quickly as possible.' His face was no longer scarred with emotion—it was the face of a hostile stranger who had won. 'We'll get married in three weeks.'

She raised her head, uneasily. What have I done? she thought intensely, and her pulses throbbed with a premonition of danger.

CHAPTER FOUR

LOUISA could hear the air vibrating with the heavy bass thud of Pete's rock group. The dark brick alleyway that led to the rehearsal studios was damp and grey. Her footsteps rang out as she made her way to the door.

The noise grew louder. Guitars whined against heavy pounding bass rhythms, the harsh crash of drums and cymbals reaching her ears. She pushed open the second door and walked into the studio.

Pete looked up, his eyes brightening for a second. The rest of the band continued playing, greeting her with silent nods as they crashed and pounded out the last few bars of the song.

Pete stepped away from the mike, pulling his guitar over his head and resting it on a chair. He came towards her, his face serious. 'What happened last night? You didn't say goodbye.'

Steve, the noisy belligerent drummer, carried on drumming, making a terrible racket.

'Pack it in!' Pete bellowed, and Steve raised his scruffy head, grinning through weeks of unshaven beard, giving a last defiant roll on the drums before stopping. Pete turned back to Louisa, frowning. 'Why didn't you call me at work today? You must have known I was waiting to hear from you.'

She avoided his eyes, shrugging. 'I was too busy,' she said, and looked back at him. 'Listen, I have to talk to you. Is there anywhere we can go?' Her eyes darted around the hollow white studio, the smoky air, stray beer cans scattered around it.

Pete studied her for a long moment, then nodded. 'Okay,' he said slowly, and his eyes narrowed as though he suspected what was on her mind. 'Hold on a minute.'

Steve was restlessly tapping his fingers on the cymbals. 'How you doing, Louisa?' he called cheerfully. 'Like the party last night? It really wiped me out—all those nice people in that nice hice.' He shook his shaggy head and gave a roll on the drums. 'Wow!' he intoned in a mock swoon.

Pete came back with his jacket and gave him a speaking glance. 'Steve, if you don't cut that out I swear I'll brain you!' he told him, taking Louisa's arm and leading her to the door. They stepped outside into the cool clean night and Louisa bit her lip, wondering how to tell him. 'Well?' Pete asked as they stood in the alleyway facing each other. 'Is it about last night? The party?'

She looked away from him anxiously. 'In a way,' she said, her voice husky. She sighed. 'It's difficult to know where to start.'

Pete raised one thin brow, his face serious. 'Try the beginning,' he suggested drily.

Louisa sighed again, then took a deep breath and haltingly began to tell him about her life before she met him. She told him everything. It was difficult at first, knowing how to phrase her meeting with Jacey, the arguments they had had. But although she stumbled once or twice, she told him everything that she could.

He deserves to know, she thought sadly. She watched his face, seeing it set without expression as he listened. When she had finished, she was silent, watching him.

'That's quite a story,' Pete said coolly, thrusting his hands into the pockets of his jeans. He looked back at her, his eyes masked. 'Sure you've told me everything?'

She nodded, her body still with anxiety as she studied him.

Pete nodded, considering this. He scuffed his worn trainers against the dark wall. 'And you've said you'll do it? Marry him?'

Louisa bit her lip, seeing the control he was exerting over himself. 'I've hurt him a great deal,' she said quietly, 'I have to make up for it.'

Pete gave a short laugh. 'Oh, poor old Jacey!' he said with bitter sarcasm. 'My heart bleeds for him!' He looked at her, his eyes no longer masked, bitter anger in their depths. 'I suppose I don't matter? I was just someone to pass the time with?'

Louisa winced. 'I'm sorry, Peter,' she said, her throat tight with guilt.

His eyes flared. 'So thanks, but no, thanks?' he said angrily. 'Is that it? Playing musical wedding rings, are we? And Jacey was the lucky winner?'

She went scarlet, then white, her eyes widening with a sense of helpless guilt. She had caused so much trouble, and she wished she could do or say something to make up for it.

She looked at him sadly. 'I'm sorry,' she repeated in a husky voice, 'I wish there was something I could do to help you understand.' She raked a hand through her hair. 'I've made such a mess of things!'

'Oh, please—spare me!' said Pete in a tight, bitter voice, his eyes flaring with anger. 'You really take the biscuit, you know that? How you have the nerve to come out with rubbish like that, I don't know. You've been playing some kind of bizarre game with both of us, haven't you? Ditch him, marry me—ditch me, marry him. What next, I wonder? Are you going to come up with some other lucky challenger?'

She winced, her face as white as chalk. 'It isn't like that!' she protested in an agonised whisper. 'I do care for you—I care very much. I just feel more for Jacey.' She bit her lip anxiously. 'It doesn't mean I didn't feel anything for you.'

'Where's my sick bag?' Pete asked bitingly. 'I think I'm going to throw up.' He considered her for a moment in a tense silence, then he said in a low, angry voice, 'I think you must be some kind of sadist. But whatever you are, I don't want any part of you. Jacey can keep you, and good luck to the poor bastard!'

He turned to push blindly past her, and she stumbled, falling against the wall. Her hand went out quickly, catching hold of his sleeve and pulling him back, her face tight with anguish.

'Don't you think I've been hurt as much as anyone else?' she whispered, tears burning the back of her eyes.

He smiled tightly. 'Frankly, my dear,' he said with biting sarcasm as he quoted the book through his teeth, 'I don't give a damn.' He looked at her stricken face and his eyes were hard. 'In my opinion, you deserve everything you get!'

Louisa slumped against the wall, watching him go. She closed her eyes as tears threatened to fight their way through. He was right: she deserved everything she was getting. It had been her own pride which had forced her into Peter's arms, and now she was paying for it.

I should have listened to Scotty, she thought with a bitter smile of grudging respect. He knew what he was talking about. Storing up trouble for yourself, he had told her, and he had been right.

She straightened, her face strained and tense. She couldn't go home to her lonely, quiet flat just yet. She needed to talk to someone. Scotty, she thought, walking along the alleyway towards the bus station; Scotty will listen.

Her reflection wavered and doubled in the night-darkened window of the bus. Louisa felt a strange sense of isolation. The top deck was deserted, the only sound that of the engine chugging, the sides rattling. She stared into space, her eyes blank. Two girls clambered up the stairs, smoking cigarettes and giggling, although they looked far too young to be smoking. They eyed Louisa with angry defiance as she looked at the cigarettes in their hands, then clattered on high heels to the back of the bus, still giggling.

Louisa got off at the next stop.

'So you haven't been kidnapped?' Scotty exclaimed with relief as he opened the front door to see her standing there.

She smiled. 'Not quite,' she admitted, following him into the quiet, rather musty-smelling house, glad of its warmth and comfort as she sat in one of the gaily patterned chairs.

She told him everything that had happened; first with Jacey, then with Pete. Scotty listened broodingly, his old mouth clenched around his pipe, his grey brows drawn in a frown of concern.

As she spoke, thoughts whirled in her head, pushing through the confused mist that seemed to surround her mind. But nothing became clearer, although she began to feel more calm about it. Scotty's presence always calmed her. She was right to have come to him.

'Don't say I told you so!' she warned after she had finished.

'Me?' said Scotty, tapping his old brown pipe against the hearth. He smiled, 'Now where would be the point in that, lassie? You knew as well as I did that this would happen. No,' he sighed, shaking his grey head, 'I won't make you look back. You've got to look forward now, try to make him forgive you. It'll be hard, but if you can do it——' he paused, eyeing her, then smiled slowly, 'well, it'll be worth it.'

Louisa folded her hands in her lap and sighed. It would certainly be worth it, because she loved Jacey deeply. But would he ever forgive her? There was a violent darkness in him that frightened her, made her worried that perhaps forgiveness wasn't in his nature.

She looked up. 'So what now?' she asked wearily.

'Well,' Scotty stood up, his muscles groaning protestingly, and rested one withered elbow on the mantelpiece, 'you've said you'll marry him, and I take it you won't change your mind?' He glanced at her, straggly brows raised. At her agreement he continued, 'So you'll have to give up your life here, and do as he says.'

Louisa's eyes were grave as they met Scotty's wise watery blue gaze. Do as he says, she thought slowly. But just how far will he push me? She wondered. Until I crack? She shivered.

He'll come back with his teeth bared, Scotty had said. And he had.

Jacey rang her the next day. She was working in the bookshop, her mind distracted and confused. Handing in her notice officially to Scotty had made everything seem more real.

Cutting ties was always painful, but it brought everything home to her with a bang. She was really leaving. Everything she had built up for herself was gradually shattering around her ears.

'Telephone!' Scotty waved the receiver at her with a grim smile, and she took it, feeling her pulses race furiously, knowing too well who was on the line.

'You told him?' Jacey's voice was cool, impersonal.

She sighed. 'Yes, Jacey, I told him.'

There was a pause. 'You sound like death,' he commented flatly. 'What's wrong? Not sleeping properly?' There was a trace of mockery in his tone that angered her.

She felt her pale mouth compress. 'The last few days have been rather hectic,' she admitted, 'to say the least.'

'The very least,' Jacey agreed in a lazy drawl, and Louisa tensed with irritation. He was laughing at her. 'I'm going away for a few days. But don't let it worry you,' he laughed unpleasantly. 'I shan't miss the wedding.'

'I'm sure you won't,' she said tightly.

'You can count on me,' he returned, mocking laughter in his voice. 'I'll let you know when I get back.'

'How thoughtful!' she said through pale, strained lips.

Laughter again. 'I try to please,' he agreed, then paused for a moment before saying coolly, 'Oh,

and I shouldn't pay any visits to friend Radcliffe—
you wouldn't like it if I found out you'd seen
him.'

Her body tensed angrily. 'Resorting to threats,
Jacey?' she asked in a soft, deliberately taunting
voice.

'Who's Jacey?' he said tightly, and hung up.

Louisa looked at the buzzing receiver with bitter
eyes for a long moment. Replacing it, she noticed
her hand shake. He's going to destroy me, she
thought angrily.

Later that day, she put Pete's ring into an
envelope and posted it to him. He wouldn't accept
it if she took it to him, she knew that. But she
couldn't keep it. Especially after the way her
engagement had been broken off. She hoped that
one day he would be able to understand why it
had happened at all. But she wasn't sure if he
would. She sighed, wishing she could turn time
back. Impossible, she realised grimly.

She saw very little of Jacey. The days passed
slowly, but when she looked back, she couldn't
understand where they had gone. She spent her
time working during the day, and sitting at home
alone in the evenings. Sometimes she went round
to see Scotty, who she thought of now as her only
friend in a nightmare world. But even he couldn't
help her now. She was trapped of her own
volition.

A week before the wedding, Jacey turned up on
her doorstep. She had had a tiring day, shifting
new deliveries of books in the shop, and hadn't
bothered to change when she had arrived home.

The sharp peremptory ring at the door told her
who it was. In her mind's eye, she could picture

him jabbing the bell with one long finger. Going downstairs, she opened the door, feeling her heart pound faster.

'You look washed out,' Jacey drawled, his panther-green eyes travelling over her face, noting the pallor of her skin, the shadows beneath her eyes. 'Too much Scotch and late nights?'

She gave him a tight smile. 'Of course.'

One dark brow rose with sardonic amusement. 'Been living it up at nightclubs in my absence?' he asked lazily, sliding his hands into the pockets of his black trousers.

Her mouth compressed angrily, as she sensed the mockery. 'You know what they say—all work and no play makes Jack a dull boy.'

Jacey gave a hard crack of laughter, showing predatory white teeth. 'Lying in your teeth, my darling.' He glanced over his shoulder, pointing with one long finger towards a small red Mini parked nearby. 'See anything familiar?' he asked.

Her eyes narrowed. The little red Mini had been there for weeks. Why the hell hadn't she noticed it? She saw the driver wave at them and felt sick to her stomach. Her skin crawled at the idea of being watched day after day.

'Your faith in me is staggering,' she said tightly, looking back at him, her eyes dark with humiliation and anger.

'Staggering,' he agreed, and the sooty lashes flickered against his hard cheek as he slid his gaze over her once more. 'I want you to meet some people.' He jangled a set of steel keys in his palm. 'Are you ready to leave now?'

She hesitated, watching him intently. 'Define

"some people",' she said after a moment, and added, 'Family? Friends?'

Jacey pursed his lips. 'Family,' he said shortly, then gave a grim smile. 'What little is left of them, anyway.' He looked at her coolly, raising one brow. 'Are you ready or not?' he asked, and Louisa compressed her lips, going upstairs for her bag before she met him a few moments later outside in the street.

Who are you? she thought intensely as they drove to the house in silence. She had begun to realise that she knew him even less than she had thought she did. All she knew was the raw Jacey.

I knew Jacey, she thought bitterly, but this is a stranger beside me. I know nothing about him, about his life before me, about his background. Her thoughts occupied her until they reached the house, and she felt even more distant from him as he handed her out of the car with a dark unsmiling face.

The elegant house was silent as they entered. Then they heard laughter from the drawing room. Jacey pushed open the white doors, and Louisa followed.

A broad athletic-looking man in his forties looked up. 'The Master Returns,' he intoned.

He looked like a Welsh mountain, or a rugby player, or both. His hair was an unruly mop of brown curls, his cheeks pink as though he'd been running non-stop for five miles. His smile was as broad as he was.

'Hello, Glen.' Jacey closed the door behind him, and cast his eye around the room. 'Been drinking my best Scotch again, I see,' he observed. 'Where's Maggie?'

Glen pulled at the neck of his beige sweater with

a thick broad hand. 'Investigating your kitchen, I believe,' he told them, and winked at Louisa. 'A great one for kitchens, is Maggie.'

Jacey's dark brows met in a frown. 'I thought I heard someone in here with you?'

Glen looked perplexed for a moment, then his brow cleared. 'Oh, I was leafing through your back copies of *Private Eye*.' He reached out to the table and waved a wad of papers at them. 'They're a real scream.' His eyes gleamed. 'I say, did you read the one about the girl in the Tottenham Court Road who took off all her . . .'

'Yes,' Jacey cut in drily. He glanced at Louisa, his face expressionless. 'Louisa, this is my cousin once removed. Glen, my fiancée, Louisa.' He preformed the introductions with a distinct lack of interest.

Glen stood up, his eyes dancing. 'Hallo, fiancée,' he said. 'You're rather gorgeous. How would you like to join the Ashthorne all-women rugby league?'

Louisa laughed, her cheeks dimpling. 'It's not quite my style,' she admitted, relieved that he was so friendly.

'Nonsense! You'd look smashing in a rugby shirt. Look at those legs!' His bushy black brows rose to unscaled heights with admiration as he eyed her legs.

Jacey tensed beside her. 'Hands off, Glen,' he said in a soft, dangerous voice, and the atmosphere changed immediately.

She could sense the tension between them, and frowned, her eyes darting from one to the other. Jacey's face was cold, hostile—menace in his eyes as he looked at his cousin.

Glen studied him. His expression was for an instant petulant, his eyes narrowing. Then he shrugged. 'No harm intended, old boy,' he drawled. 'Just flattering the young lady.'

Jacey watched him with narrowed eyes, then he nodded curtly. 'I'm going to find that piranha you married.' He opened the door and gave them a tight smile. 'I shouldn't be long.'

The tension, Louisa thought—there has to be a reason for the tension. Looking at Glen, she felt her eyes narrow thoughtfully. Why had Jacey overreacted to his cousin's compliments?

'So you're the latest to join the clan,' Glen said with a hint of acidity, his head tilted to one side. 'What do you think of us so far? And don't give the obvious answer!'

Louisa watched him, then smiled slowly. 'I haven't met all of you, yet,' she said, choosing her words carefully. 'Are there many more?'

Glen laughed, his pink cheeks creasing. 'Not really, darling. Plenty of hangers-on—but they're not all relatives.' He downed the last of his Scotch. 'No, we're the only ones who are strictly related to the great Master.'

Louisa considered this with a frown. The door clicked open behind her, and she turned, waiting.

A short, very solid woman bustled in with a face like a deranged chicken. 'My dear!' she exclaimed in loud tones, and advanced briskly on Louisa, her hand outstretched. 'I'm so glad to meet you.' She peered at her, and frowned. 'But you're not as pretty as I'd expected. I thought he'd drag some glamour-puss home, but you're less artificial ... sort of classical.'

Louisa shook hands with her, trying to smile

graciously at this backhanded compliment. 'You must be Maggie,' she said, trying to smile naturally.

'Must I?' Maggie cocked an eyebrow. She settled down on the armchair, regarding Louisa with bright, slightly mad eyes. 'I hope you're not offended, my dear. I live by the truth.'

Glen sat down opposite her, and gave a broad smile. 'She'll die by it one of these days,' he told Louisa with a slightly barbed smile. 'She offends all my contacts. It's absolutely hopeless—the minute she opens her mouth I lose thousands of pounds!'

Maggie's eyes cut right through him. For such a short woman, with such a homely, cuddly appearance, she was surprisingly sharp. Louisa could imagine her tongue slicing through anyone.

'You could do with losing a few more,' Maggie told her husband with a glance at his rather ample waistline. 'Jason, my dear——' she patted Jacey's hand lovingly, 'so glad you decided to marry at last. Makes one so much more stable.'

'And henpecked,' Glen muttered into his glass.

Maggie looked at Jacey with raised brows. 'Your influence, I'm afraid.'

Jacey slid his hands in his pockets, his dark face expressionless. 'All the sins of the world fall on my head,' he drawled, sliding a glance at Louisa from beneath his thick dark lashes.

'Who was it,' Maggie enquired, 'who charged off like a teenager? In search of a better life, I believe you said. Leaving my Glen in charge of the business—and interfering like hell every time you deigned to make a reappearance?'

Louisa listened carefully to each word. She

looked across at Jacey. So he was the head of a business. That was something she hadn't known, something he hadn't told her. Was that why he left me all those months ago? she wondered.

Jacey was watching Maggie with narrowed eyes. 'You know damned well why I went,' he said softly, and Louisa again sensed the tension in the atmosphere.

Maggie laughed, clasping her hands beneath her ample bosom. 'Oh yes, we all know why,' she said, eyes bright and a little feverish. 'But surely you should have waited for a decent interval to elapse?' She looked across at Louisa. 'I mean, so soon after Rachel . . .'

'That's enough!' Jacey's softly spoken words created an atmosphere of highly charged tension. Louisa noticed Glen stiffen as she watched him. What the hell is going on? she thought, her eyes narrowing.

Maggie's eyes were hostile, the madness brighter. 'I would have thought one wife was enough for you, but no . . .'

Jacey's glass smashed on the table as he stood up. 'I said enough!' he bit out between his teeth.

Louisa stared at him, incredulous. 'Who,' she asked under her breath, 'is Rachel?'

Dinner was unbearable. Maggie's words ran through her mind constantly as she tried to fit them all together. What had happened to Rachel? Who was she, and where was she now? She glanced at Jacey from time to time, needing desperately to ask him, yet not knowing quite how to. It was all so painful for her. She felt afraid of him, and knew she shouldn't. Lovers should be friends, too, she thought sadly, not enemies. She didn't want a marriage built on a foundation of lies and hatred. She wanted Jacey back, the man she had fallen in love with so long ago. How everything had changed since that first sweet meeting, she thought, sighing.

When Glen and Maggie finally left, Louisa sat in the drawing room with Jacey, feeling uneasy as she plucked up the courage to speak to him.

'Who is Rachel?' she asked quietly as they sat on the settee together.

Jacey glanced at her slowly, and the dark lashes flickered as he held her gaze. She searched his eyes for a sign of emotion, for a sign of the old feelings which had once been there for her.

'My wife.'

Her heart stopped then thrust at her chest painfully. 'Your *wife*?'

'She's dead now,' he said quietly, and sighed, pursing his lips. 'Died a few months ago.'

Louisa's pulses drummed in her ears. 'Your wife,' she breathed. 'You were married when I met you! All that time we spent together—and it meant nothing to you!' She couldn't believe it, couldn't bear to think of all the words they had said to each other, which she thought he'd meant . . . and all the time he was married to another woman! She stared at him in disbelief. 'You were using me!'

'No!' He stood up, staring down at her, his face brooding. Then he pushed his hands into his pockets and gave a harsh sigh. 'She left me three years ago. Or I threw her out—I can never remember which it was.'

She could hardly believe her ears. 'You can't remember?' She shook her head, staring at him incredulously. 'Your own wife? And you can't remember how it ended?' Slowly, she stood up too, clutching her fingers at her waist. 'Is that what's in store for me? The minute you're fed up with me, will I be out on my ear too?'

Jacey ran a hand through his thick black hair, sliding a glance at her with impatient eyes. 'She was a cheap little tramp,' he muttered. 'She went to bed with anyone at the drop of a hat. I put up with it for as long as I could, then I threw her out.' He drew a deep breath, his eyes meeting hers for a long moment. 'I'm not made of stone, Louisa. I have my pride.'

'You have too much pride,' she muttered, bending her head. They were both too proud—and although the pride was a part of their strength, she knew it would destroy them in the end.

'Likewise, Louisa,' he muttered, his eyes stormy. He slid one hand over her slender neck, pressing his thumb and forefinger into her throat. 'I'll break your pride, though. I'll have you on your knees before I'm through!'

She raised her eyes to his, refusing to back down. 'That's not my style, Jacey. I don't beg from any man.'

'*Not Jacey!*' He slammed his hand on the table, eyes blazing, and she jumped as his hands closed over her throat. '*How many times do I have to tell you?*' he asked thickly. '*Do I have to smash it into that thick skull of yours?*'

'Is that why she left you?' Louisa asked angrily, facing him, her temper clashing with his as she stood her ground. 'Did you have to smash it through her skull too?'

'No,' he bit out. 'Rachel would have enjoyed it

too much.' He gave a harsh laugh, his sharp white
teeth exposed, but the smile didn't reach his eyes. 'I
seem to have sadistic patterns. I tend to pick women
who enjoy too much sex and too much violence.'

Louisa sucked her breath in, the colour draining
from her face.

Jacey slid one hand to her neck, the fingers tight
on her flesh. 'Is that what really turns you on, my
darling?' he drawled tightly, and pulled her
towards him, his hard lean body making heat rush
through her. 'Rough trade?'

'Don't touch me!' she said breathlessly, panic
making her heart race wildly inside her, thrusting
at her breast, her pulses drumming frenziedly in
her ears.

His mouth clamped shut like a steel trap.
'Sorry,' he said, his voice stinging, 'I forgot. Men
don't turn you on, do they? It's power that does
the trick. Power and money.' He watched her, his
eyes lancing her with bitter contempt. He was
breathing hard, his heart thudding at his rib cage.
'Well, I'll give you what turns you on. But first I
want to make sure I'm getting my money's worth.'

Louisa felt her heart stop. She swayed against
him, the blood pulsating around her body as he
pressed her against him, his long fingers sliding
over her, touching her, making her heart race.

'Before you get my money,' Jacey muttered
thickly, 'I want to make sure we're compatible.'
His eyes burned on her mouth, his breathing
quickening. 'In bed.'

Her eyes widened with breathless panic as his
mouth came closer and closer. His lips clamped
down over hers, and she clung to him, her
emotions out of control.

His hot mouth moved frenziedly over her, his hands sliding over her, pressing her harder against him. Louisa groaned helplessly and her fingers slid to his head, tangling in his thick black hair, pulling him closer and closer.

She could barely breathe. It had been so long since he had kissed her, and her need for him combined with the violent force of their emotions to create a frenzy inside both of them.

Jacey lifted his head, breathing raggedly. 'Upstairs,' he muttered, his eyes half closed, glittering through heavy lids.

She swayed against him, her eyes glazed. 'Let me go, Jacey,' she said in a rough unsteady voice. 'Let me go or I'll back out altogether. I won't marry you if you force me to do it.'

There was a long tense silence. She watched him intently, hoping he wouldn't fight. The time wasn't right for lovemaking. She couldn't possibly let him make love to her knowing how much he hated and despised her; it would hurt too much.

'Very well,' said Jacey flatly after a short pause, 'I suppose I can wait. I can always divorce you if you're no good.'

She sucked her breath in incredulously. 'Have you no feelings?' she gasped, her face white.

'Not any more,' he said tightly.

She looked at him, her throat stinging. Nothing's turned out the way it should have done, she thought bitterly. Nothing ever does. I held happiness in the palm of my hand, and I threw it away for pride and vanity's sake. All she had left were hopes that one day Jacey would be able to forgive her.

Would I forgive him? Louisa asked herself, and

knew the answer already. Pride had caused the situation they found themselves in now. They were both too proud, too strong.

Over the months, she had lost her strength. Mistrust and confusion had sapped it, leaving her weak and malleable, hurt and bewildered. Now she had to find it again and put it to good use.

If she didn't, Jacey would destroy her.

CHAPTER FIVE

SCOTTY plied her with sherry on her last day at work. It was only fitting, he told her calmly, that she should celebrate her last day at work. Last day of independence, thought Louisa as she watched him pour the smooth liquid into a crystal glass. Once she stopped work, her income would stop, and she would be totally dependent on Jacey.

The idea didn't bear thinking about. The man she remembered had gone, replaced by a menacing stranger, and Louisa wasn't sure that she could cope with him. If she cared nothing for him it would be easy; but loving him the way she did put a different accent on their relationship and the balance of power was bound to swing in his favour.

'Here,' Scotty handed her a glass of sherry, 'one more for the road.'

'Lucky road,' she said brightly, sipping it.

Scotty raised his glass in a silent toast. He sighed. 'What'll I do when you're gone?' He turned kind blue eyes to look at her. 'Three years you've been here. Won't be the same without you.'

'I should hope not,' Louisa teased gently. 'I like to think of myself as memorable.'

He chuckled into his glass. 'I remember when you first came here. What a mess you made of the accounts! Worse than useless.'

Her cheeks dimpled. 'I was very penitent, though.'

'Under age, too,' he said, eyeing her wryly, 'I should never have employed you. Even with those clever black eyes you didn't look twenty.'

She wrinkled her nose. 'You don't have to be twenty to work in bookshops.'

Scotty pinched her ear. 'I distinctly remember asking for someone over twenty in the advertisement.' He watched her for a moment with a smile. 'But you didn't do too badly.'

'Thank you, kind sir,' she said gravely, and Scotty grinned, smacking her on the wrist. Louisa's eyes were affectionate as she studied him, remembering how much she owed him. When she had first arrived in London, she had had no home, no friends, and no money.

Thanks to Scotty she hadn't been starved out of the West End. He had known instinctively that she was desperate for work, and she had been able to find her feet because of his generosity, able to build a life away from home.

The shop door opened and they both looked up as the bell jangled. Louisa tensed, her fingers clutching the sherry glass tightly as she watched him walk in slowly.

Pete was dressed in the same tatty jeans and sneakers he had worn when she first met him. But this time, his face wore a grim expression, his eyes no longer filled with warmth and amusement.

'Hallo, Pete,' she said anxiously, studying him.

He nodded curtly. 'Louisa.' Stopping at the counter, he reached into his jeans pockets and pulled out the ring she had returned to him. 'I came to return this,' he told her.

The ring flashed as he held it up and she looked at it, biting her lip. Then she raised her eyes to his.

'It's not mine any more, Pete,' she said quietly.

His thin brows rose. 'Do you expect me to wear it?'

Louisa looked at the ring as he laid it with a snap on the counter. Then slowly she held out her left hand, moving the third finger. Jacey's engagement ring glittered on her slender finger, the simple diamond solitaire elegant and beautiful.

'I already have one,' she pointed out softly, and she knew it would hurt him, knew it would push a thorn home inside. But it was better to make the break between them as quick and painless as possible.

Pete looked at the ring bitterly. 'Rich, is he?'

She flushed. 'That isn't why I'm marrying him, Pete.'

'No, of course not,' he said under his breath. 'It's love, true love, the radiant bride and all that.'

'I told you—I hurt him badly, and I want to try and make up for it . . .'

'Do go on,' he muttered, eyes accusing, 'and on, and on, and on!'

There was a long silence. Louisa looked steadily at the ring, watching it reflect light as it lay on the white-topped counter, hoping he would pick it up. She didn't want him hurt any more. But he was making it very difficult for her to end it with one quick break.

She moistened her lips. 'I'm sorry this had to happen, Pete, I wish it could have been different . . .'

'Oh, shut up!' he snapped angrily, then broke off, pushing a hand through his hair.

She lapsed into silence, her fingers restless on the counter as she tried to think of something else to say. But what could she say? Nothing.

Pete was watching her, his eyes angry. Then he sighed, leaning against the counter. 'Why?' he asked under his breath, staring at the floor. He looked back at her. 'Why have you done this?'

She looked up hopelessly. 'I love him.'

Pete drew an unsteady breath. 'Hell!' he muttered, taking the ring and stuffing it into his jeans pocket before turning to walk out of the shop.

But the door opened before he reached it. Jacey stood in the doorway, his eyes darting from Louisa to Pete and back again. He tensed for a moment, standing deadly still, then he closed the door behind him.

'Well, well, well,' he drawled unpleasantly, 'if it isn't our wealthy friend!' He looked at Louisa with narrowed eyes. 'What the hell is he doing here?'

Pete was perplexed, frowning uneasily. He looked Jacey up and down, his face showing the fact that he didn't quite understand what was going on. Then he looked over his shoulder at Louisa with a puzzled frown.

'Who is this guy?' he asked her slowly.

'This guy,' Jacey drawled before Louisa could speak, 'is the man she's going to marry.'

Realisation dawned on Pete's face. 'So you're Jacey,' he said curiously. 'No wonder she prefers you to me—you've got money written all over you. I'm just a poor relation compared to you.'

'Watch your mouth, Radcliffe!' Jacey gritted tightly.

Pete ignored him. 'So the best man won! Lucky old you. But I shouldn't go counting any chickens. She's marrying you out of pity—did you know that? Feels sorry for you. 'Poor Jacey,' he mimicked, and Louisa flushed—it was a brilliant imitation of her voice.

Jacey pushed away from the door, his body tense, hostile. 'Get out before I knock your teeth down your throat,' he muttered under his breath.

Pete laughed at him, which only made Jacey angrier. 'The truth hurts, does it?' he said, thin brows raised. 'I wouldn't lay any bets on how long she'll stay, either. The word faithful doesn't enter her vocabulary.'

Jacey's jaw tightened. 'You really ask for it, don't you?' he said tightly, moving towards him.

Louisa was out from behind the counter in two seconds flat. 'Jacey, don't!' She clutched at his arm desperately.

He looked down at her in surprise, his eyes searching hers for a long moment in silence. She felt her heart thudding faster as she watched him anxiously.

'I'm not letting him get away with that!' he said angrily.

She shook her head. 'He doesn't mean any of it. He's just angry and hurt—surely you can see that?'

Jacey studied her for a long moment, then his muscles relaxed slowly. He turned to Pete. 'All right, Radcliffe,' he said grimly, 'clear off. And think yourself lucky I don't push your face into the middle of next week!'

'My pleasure.' Pete muttered, obviously shaken, and went out of the door quickly, slamming it behind him, making the bell jangle furiously.

Louisa sighed, relieved that nothing had happened. There was a darkness in Jacey that worried her. She had unleashed it by betraying him, in his eyes, and she was very much afraid that she had unleashed a violent jealousy in him at the same time. What frightened her most was that the darkness in him clicked inside her, and only served to intensify her own feelings towards him.

Perhaps it was the fierce possessiveness that made her feel secure. After all, if he wanted her this badly, it was pretty obvious that he wasn't going to let go of her again if he could help it. A classic case of the thunderbolt, she thought, looking up at him.

She found he was watching her intently, almost as though his eyes were branding her with his name, and she flushed under that steady gaze. 'It's just the way he feels at the moment,' she said quietly. 'He'll get over it.'

Jacey's eyes were stormy. 'I sure hope so!' he muttered under his breath. 'If I find I've married another Rachel . . .' He let the words dance in the air with an unspoken threat, and Louisa knew that at that moment he would kill anyone who took her away from him again.

The thought sent a frisson of electricity through her. The power of his feeling fuelled her own. She hoped their need would only grow instead of fizzling out.

Jacey held a small party three days before the wedding. He wanted her to meet some friends, he said, but Louisa thought he was putting the penultimate stamp of ownership on her. Parading her in front of his friends would only bring the reality of it all home to her.

He had bought her an extensive new wardrobe. Louisa had felt foolish as he led her into the expensive Bond Street shop and picked out a

A SUPERROMANCE™
the great new romantic novel she never wanted to end. And it can be yours
FREE!

She never wanted it to end. And neither will you. From the moment you begin… *Love Beyond Desire,* your **FREE** introduction to the newest series of bestseller romance novels, **SUPERROMANCES**.

You'll be enthralled by this powerful love story… from the moment Robin meets the dark, handsome Carlos an finds herself involved in the jealousies, bitterness an secret passions of the Lopez family. Where her own forbidden love threatens to shatter her life.

Your FREE *Love Beyond Desire* is only the beginning. A subscription to **SUPERROMANCES** lets you look forward to a long love affair. Month after mont you'll receive four love stories of heroic dimension. Novels that will involve you in spellbinding intrigue, forbidden love and fiery passions.

You'll begin this series of sensuous, exciting contemporary novels… written by some of the top romance novelists of the day… with four each month

And this big value… each novel, almost 400 pages of compelling reading… is yours for only $2.5(book. Hours of entertainment for so little. Far less tha a first-run movie or Pay-TV. Newly published novels, with beautifully illustrated covers, filled with page aft page of delicious escape into a world of romantic love… delivered right to your home.

A compelling love story of mystery and intrigue... conflicts and jealousies... and a forbidden love that threatens to shatter the lives of all involved with the aristocratic Lopez family.

← Mail this card today for your FREE gifts.

TAKE THIS BOOK AND TOTE BAG FREE!

Mail to: SUPERROMANCE
2504 W. Southern Avenue, Tempe, Arizona 85282

YES, please send me FREE and without any obligation, my **SUPERROMANCE** novel, *Love Beyond Desire.* If you do not hear from me after I have examined my FREE book, please send me the 4 new **SUPERROMANCE** books every month as soon as they come off the press. I understand that I will be billed only $2.50 per book (total $10.00). There are no shipping and handling or any other hidden charges. There is no minimum number of books that I have to purchase. In fact, I may cancel this arrangement at any time. *Love Beyond Desire* and the tote bag are mine to keep as FREE gifts even if I do not buy any additional books.

134-CIS-KAE4

Name	(Please Print)

Address	Apt. No.

City

State	Zip

Signature   (If under 18, parent or guardian must sign.)

This offer is limited to one order per household and not valid to present subscribers. We reserve the right to exercise discretion in granting membership. If price changes are necessary you will be notified. Offer expires December 31, 1983.

SUPERROMANCE ™

PRINTED IN U.S.A.

**EXTRA BONUS
MAIL YOUR ORDER
TODAY AND GET A
FREE TOTE BAG
FROM SUPERROMANCE.**

↢ Mail this card today for your FREE gifts.

whole row of exquisite clothes for her. The prices had made her breath catch with incredulity—the dress she was wearing now had cost more than two months' wages.

Jacey came up behind her and his eyes met hers in the gilt-edged mirror. 'Enjoying yourself?' he asked smokily, his long fingers sliding over her throat, and the cool touch made her shiver, pulses leaping.

She nodded, smiling a little. 'I like your friends—most of them.'

His brows linked with amused enquiry. 'Most of them?'

Louisa looked at him through her lashes. 'Some of them aren't quite real.' She saw his answering smile and knew he agreed with her. The people in the other room were on the whole natural and friendly, but one or two spoilt the atmosphere with pretence, hiding behind glossy masks and false smiles.

Louisa hated people like that. How could you talk to someone if they hid behind an image all the time? It was like talking to beautiful marble statues, or being a teenager again and kissing posters goodnight.

The doorbell rang and she turned. Their faces were inches away from each other, and Louisa felt her breath catch as her eyes fell on his firm mouth. The sensuality was almost overpowering.

Stepping past him, she felt her pulses race as she walked to the door, sensing his eyes burning into the back of her neck as she walked away from him.

It was Glen and Maggie, standing on the threshold, their faces flushed.

'I come in peace,' Glen announced, holding up his hand like an American Indian.

Louisa laughed lightly. 'So I should hope!'

Maggie thrust a bottle of brandy into her hands. 'Where's Jason?' she asked briskly, pushing past Louisa and marching into the hall.

Louisa glanced over her shoulder. 'Mingling, I expect.'

Glen jiggled his bushy black brows and grinned. 'That sounds fun. Do you mingle?'

'Not with rugby players. I'm not much good in a scrum.'

Glen laughed, flattered. 'You've got a good memory!'

She smiled and moved away, the exquisite black silk dress rustling at her feet. Sensual and elegant, it clung like a second skin, the diamanté-studded straps crossing over her bare back, the material slashed to the waist at the back. Long black evening gloves lent seductive highlights, showing creamy white skin where they ended. A diamond bracelet flashed at her wrist over the black gloves like frost.

Jacey stepped into the doorway of the drawing room just as she walked towards it. His gaze swept her possessively, and she tilted her head to meet it. She felt a little uncomfortable in such elegant surroundings, but she didn't let it show.

Someone had once said—'Sex appeal is half what you've got and half what you make other people think you've got'—and Louisa stuck to that like glue. It could be applied to anything from sex appeal to courage to personality. Confidence, she decided, is definitely half.

'Jason, my dear!' Maggie bustled up to him,

resplendent in a shocking pink dress, her bosom spilling over the top, several gaudy bracelets clanking at her wrists. 'So glad you're introducing Louisa to everyone. One does approve.'

'One does one's best,' Jacey drawled, imitating wickedly.

Louisa hid a smile—he was a brilliant mimic.

Maggie decided not to notice. 'Rachel was so frightfully difficult to get to know—always hiding behind that silly image. I do hope Louisa has more sense.'

Jacey's jaw tightened, his eyes narrowing.

Glen interceded quickly. 'Do stop putting on your party voice, darling,' he muttered, gripping his wife's arm and dragging her away. 'It clashes with your dress.'

Maggie hissed something very rude as Glen led her off, and Louisa watched with amusement. Maggie looked like a mad chicken turned punk rocker!

Jacey was watching Louisa shrewdly. 'You look pale,' he said tersely. 'Did they say anything to upset you?'

She frowned. 'What could they have said, Jacey?'

His face shuttered. 'Nothing.' He slid an arm around her waist and began to lead her away, his fingers splaying on her hips as her body moved sinuously against him.

She shook a dozen hands and met a dozen faces, but they all faded into an indiscriminate blur. In the end, she escaped, exhausted, to look for peace and quiet in the kitchen.

Jacey was on her mind, as always, and she stared blankly ahead as she walked into the quiet kitchen. Jacey again, she thought, closing her eyes. She suddenly felt angry with herself. Is that all I am? Jacey's partner? Don't I belong to myself any more, don't I exist without him? She sighed, closing the door a little and sipping the last of her drink.

She noticed Glen in the corner by the fridge. He was trapped by an anaemic-looking woman with garish red hair and great slabs of blue eye make-up on.

'The kids have just had flu,' the redhead was droning in a flat, boring voice, 'and my husband's been limping for weeks. He tripped over the cat.'

'Louisa!' Glen saw her with relief. 'Have you met Deirdre?'

Deirdre turned her red head and looked at her with bloodshot eyes. 'I shouldn't come too close,' she said in a dead voice, 'I've just had bronchitis.'

Glen made a tragedian gesture, his mouth forming a silent howl.

Louisa tried not to smile. Deirdre had to be heard to be believed. 'I thought I'd have some more punch,' Louisa said casually.

Glen jumped away from Deirdre like a shot. 'Good idea!'

'I must go and take my pills,' said Deirdre, disappearing.

Glen groaned with relief. 'Oh, that woman! My back teeth have just been bored out of their sockets!'

Louisa spooned the thick punch into her glass and sipped it. Her lids closed with a sigh as the cool air from the kitchen window touched her hot cheeks. It was so peaceful out here.

She looked back at Glen with a smile. 'I thought

she was quite nice,' she murmured, laughing under her breath.

Glen pulled a face. 'If you like hearing private instalments of *General Hospital*! I dread to think what it's like to live with her. They probably paint a red cross on the door and ring a bell outside shouting "Unclean, unclean"!'

Louisa laughed, her dark eyes sparkling with amusement. Looking out of the window, she felt a sigh escape her at the beauty of the night. Little silver stars twinkled like moondust in the dark blue night, filling the air with romance. Her mouth turned down at the corners. If only Jacey still loved me, she thought, this would be so perfect.

'Penny for them,' Glen nudged her arm with a grin.

She turned, smiling. 'That's so corny, it's almost edible!'

'You looked sad,' Glen said quietly. He shrugged, pretending indifference. 'I thought I could help. But obviously you're Superwoman, so I'll leave you to search your inner self with X-ray vision.'

He turned to go, and Louisa caught at his sleeve, frowning. She hadn't meant to offend him. He had only been trying to help. He looked back, and she gave him a quick, apologetic smile. 'Sorry.'

Glen watched her for a long moment, his eyes shrewd. 'It's Jason, is it?' he asked softly, and she looked away, suddenly caught between asking him to tell her more about Jacey, and telling him not to talk to her. Jacey wouldn't be pleased, to say the least, if he knew she was discussing him with his cousin. But what else could she do? Jacey wasn't going to tell her any more than he had to.

Glen read the hesitation in her eyes. 'I'll tell you about Rachel, if you like,' he said slowly, watching her, and she nodded, biting her lip. Why not? Glen perched on a kitchen stool, nursing his drink. 'Rachel was very pretty, very sexy, very spoilt, and probably the most selfish person I ever met.'

Louisa eyed him. 'You didn't like her?' That made her frown, because she had got the feeling that Glen had liked Rachel. Nothing had been said, but all the same, she had picked up that feeling somehow.

Glen stiffened, looking away. 'Not much,' he murmured, then downed the last of his drink before saying, 'Anyway, Jason found out she was seeing half the male population of London and went berserk—threw her out.'

'Was he very violent with her?'

'He didn't hit her, if that's what you mean. It was all very dramatic—you know, never darken my doorstep, and that kind of thing. But he didn't divorce her, just bought her a house in California and sent her packing.'

She listened intently. 'How long ago was this?'

He frowned. 'Three years or so. As soon as she left, Jason pushed off too. Left the business, left the house—everything, and just took the clothes he stood up in. We rarely saw him after that.'

So Jacey had been living alone in London for a long time before she met him. Now I know what he meant when he said he was sick of the world he lived in, Louisa thought. A wife who ran around town with other men, and who only wanted him for his money. That wasn't much of a life for any man.

'Rachel came back a few months ago,' Glen continued. 'She wanted Jason to give her some more money. He wasn't here, though—no one knows where he was.'

He was with me, she thought, her heart hurting. Tears were stinging her eyes, so she closed them, refusing to cry in front of Glen. I should have trusted him, she thought, angry with herself. I should have waited until he felt able to trust me. Instead, she had let him down when he needed her most.

'Rachel didn't give up easily, though,' Glen was saying with a smile. 'She worked on Jason's father to get the money out of him. And one day she took him for a drive.'

There was a silence, and Louisa looked up sharply, sensing the unspoken words before they came. 'What happened?' she asked.

Glen sipped his drink. 'Rachel drove them both into a tree. They died on impact.'

She gasped, horrified. 'How terrible!' She thought, no wonder Jacey hates me so much! His emotions towards her were tied up inexorably with the death of his father and of his ex-wife. Just when he needed her support, she had betrayed him. But surely the hatred stemmed from love? The opposite of love is indifference, not hatred. Hatred is raw emotion—surely she could change it back into love if she worked at it, proved to him that he had never really left her thoughts?

Glen was shrugging. 'I liked old Mr Knight—he was a good guy. But Rachel wrecked everything she touched—her middle name was trouble.'

'I can't believe anyone could be as bad as all that,' Louisa sighed.

Glen laughed. 'You didn't know Rachel. She was the absolute pits!'

Rachel had obviously been a destructive woman, Louisa realised. Is that how Jacey is beginning to see me too? she thought with sudden sadness. She had certainly wrecked their chances by being faithless. His wife and father had died tragically, and instead of trusting him she had thought only of herself.

That was the trouble with being insecure. When you're insecure you only ever see things from your own angle. Jacey had been sad, depressed, and instead of seeing he was in trouble, she had thought the sadness in his eyes had been an indication that he was no longer interested in her.

'Hey!' Glen said gently, sliding an arm around her, concerned. 'Don't worry—it'll be okay.'

Louisa realised with a shock that she had been crying, and did her best to calm down, wiping her damp eyes with a trembling hand.

Glen stiffened suddenly, turning his head.

'Get away from her,' Jacey drawled, standing deathly still in the doorway, and Louisa looked up sharply, her eyes widening. Not again, she thought.

'No can do, chum.' Glen looked obstinate. 'She's upset.'

Jacey laughed—a hollow, angry laugh. 'Are you crazy?' he drawled icily. 'Rachel didn't want you— what makes you think Louisa will?'

Glen turned scarlet, then white, his face draining of colour. His eyes stared blankly at Jacey, and Louisa suddenly knew why the atmosphere was so tense whenever Jacey saw her with him. Glen's arm dropped from her shoulder and he walked stiffly out of the room.

There was a long silence. Louisa watched Jacey warily, wondering why he hadn't told her about Glen and Rachel before.

'Stay away from him,' Jacey said tightly, and swung away without another word.

She stared at the empty doorway in angry disbelief. He just walked away, every time, without explaining anything to her, and she started to follow him, her heart thudding. It's about time I had some answers, she thought, her mouth tight. But as she reached the doorway to the drawing room she stopped, seeing Jacey.

His black head was bent in conversation with a ravishing blonde who was looking up at him, big blue eyes eating him. Louisa gritted her teeth. Jacey turned his head and their eyes met as his face shuttered, blocking her out of his thoughts and feelings.

Louisa turned away. What was the point?

The conversation with Glen haunted her. Every person she met saw Jacey with different eyes, and their words lent a new insight into his character, and what had happened to form that character. But more and more she was coming to realise that the Jacey she had first met and fallen in love with had been the man he really was, the raw Jacey, with no masks, no pretences, nothing to hide behind.

And now? She sighed, angry with herself. She had helped to drive him back into the world he had escaped from, and gradually he was re-erecting all the old barriers, the old masks. She had to help him stop it before it was too late. It was the barrier that was stopping her reaching inside him again, getting through to him.

Jacey came for her the night before the wedding to help her move her things out of the flat.

'What have you got in here?' he asked as he struggled with an enormous blue suitcase. 'A corpse?'

She shook her head, smiling tentatively.

'Two corpses?' he asked, brows raised with amusement.

She laughed, watching as he bumped it down the stairs with difficulty, the suitcase pulling him along afterwards as though it was a huge dog straining at the leash.

'Where am I supposed to put it?' Jacey complained, scratching the back of his neck as he surveyed the overflowing boot of his car. He sighed, dumping it into the back seat of the car and trying to secure it.

'Put a seat-belt on it,' Louisa suggested, peering into the car, and he laughed, looking up at her.

Their eyes met and fused. Louisa felt her pulses leap at the warmth in his smile. She hoped for one moment that he might reach out and kiss her, but he looked away.

'Is this absolutely necessary?' Jacey asked, eyeing the Chinese lampshade she handed him.

'Scotty gave it to me,' she said, refusing to leave it behind.

He sighed, exasperated, and did his best to find a place for it. Louisa didn't want to leave it behind. Poor little thing, she thought, looking at it with a smile. It looked so forlorn sitting alone in the back of the car.

'Right.' Jacey firmly put her in the front of the car. 'Nothing else, and that's final. This car already looks like a junk shop as it is.'

They drove to his house, and unloaded all her possessions. They looked, she had to admit, rather out of place in the elegant surroundings. Her ornaments mainly consisted of small fluffy toys, and they did *not* go down well put next to Dresden china and Georgian silver. She tried adjusting them, but it didn't seem to work.

'I need some coffee after that lot,' Jacey announced, going into the kitchen. 'How about you?'

She followed him in, cradling her small collection of crockery in her arms. Looking in the cupboards, she realised it was going to be even more out of place. She put most of it back into boxes to be thrown away, but placed her favourite mug on the shelf.

Jacey reached for some cups, and stopped, gazing at it. 'Yours, I presume?' he said wryly, lifting it down and looking at the brightly coloured star-sign insignia. 'Sagittarius,' he remarked, reading from the mug. 'Restless, idealistic, honest, generous.'

Their eyes met. 'That's me,' said Louisa, smiling slightly.

One brow rose. 'Really?' he drawled, putting it back.

She bit her lip, looking away. The white kitchen seemed too clean, too neat. Everything was put away perfectly, the walls shining, the floor shining. She wondered where the housekeeper was. She probably spent her whole life slaving away in this kitchen.

'You haven't invited your parents to the wedding,' Jacey said suddenly, and she froze, avoiding his eyes. He studied her, arms folded across his powerful chest. 'Why?'

Louisa ran her fingers over the immaculate

surface. 'I couldn't get in touch with them,' she said huskily.

He looked at her consideringly. 'Or you didn't want to,' he suggested.

Louisa flushed and looked away. Why did he have to ask questions like this? It was really none of his business. If he could be secretive, so could she.

'And that's all I'm going to get out of you,' he drawled with a barbed smile. 'Exactly nothing.'

She raised her eyes to his, her expression grave. 'It's none of your business,' she pointed out quietly.

His mouth tightened. There was a flash of anger in his eyes. 'Very well,' he snapped, banging cups, 'be secretive!'

That did make her angry. She stared at the back of his black head and wanted to break something over it. What right had he to accuse her of that—what right had he to poke and pry into her personal life when he gave her absolutely nothing of his?

'Secretive?' she echoed angrily, staring at him. 'Me?' She drew a deep breath. 'What about you? You didn't tell me about your wife. You didn't tell me Glen had had an affair with her. In fact, you didn't tell me anything—ever!'

He looked at her over his shoulder. 'Why should Glen bother you?' he asked, frowning. 'Glen and Rachel's fling has nothing to do with you.'

She shrugged and looked away, a frown deepening in her forehead. 'It's just another secret,' she said wearily, 'just another thing to surprise me.'

He studied her coolly for a long moment, then

he slid his hands in his pockets. 'Okay. Glen got involved up to his neck with my wife, fell like a ton of bricks. But she wasn't interested—so that was that.'

'Poor Glen,' Louisa said with feeling, biting her lip.

She remembered his stricken look, the pain in his eyes. He must have suffered. Then she remembered Maggie and the way she talked about Rachel. Poor Maggie, she thought wryly.

'Poor Glen!' Jacey muttered irritably, staring at her. 'It was his own stupid fault. Our marriage had been over for years—it was an open secret, everyone knew what she was like. It was a monumental mistake.'

She looked up, her black eyes afraid. 'And us, Jacey?' she asked huskily. 'Will that happen to us, too?'

His eyes met hers grimly. 'That all depends on you.'

Her mouth tightened. 'It takes two,' she pointed out in an angry tone, watching him across the room.

His jaw clenched. 'We had a good thing going, till you broke it up.' He gave her a tight smile. 'Now you'll have to try and stick it back together again.'

Her eyes flashed angrily. 'You're not helping much!'

'Why the hell should I?' he said roughly, and she saw the tension in his body, saw the lean muscles tauten as he spoke. She was taken aback for a split second, then found her courage.

'I'm sick of her name!' she said under her breath. 'I'm sick of hearing about Rachel!'

Jacey laughed, his white teeth sharp, cutting. He studied her with an unpleasant smile. 'Jealousy,' he observed in a tight drawl.

Louisa was breathing hard, her face angry. 'I'm not made of stone!'

'Aren't you?' he said bitingly.

She heard her heart thudding very fast. The silence wrapped around her as she stared at him, unable to believe what he had said. She hadn't believed he disliked her that much.

Putting a hand to her hot cheeks, she said, 'I can't go on like this, Jacey.' Her eyes lifted to his. 'Every time we speak to each other you snipe at me.'

'How sad!' he said nastily, eyes cruel.

The black eyes flashed a warning. 'I mean it!' she said in an angry voice. 'Stop hurting me! It won't get us anywhere.'

'No?' he asked through tight, bloodless lips. 'You think you don't deserve it?'

She winced, looking away. 'Okay,' she said bitterly, 'maybe I do. But you're hurting yourself as much as me.' Her eyes searched his in desperation. 'Can't you see that?'

Suddenly she saw the hell in his eyes as he stared at her. 'Can't you?' he said hoarsely.

Her breath caught in the back of her throat. She made a strangled noise, reaching out one trembling white hand to him, needing him to make that last move, to reach out his hand to her.

Jacey groaned, moving forward. He swept her into his arms, his mouth covering hers in a draining, burning kiss. His fingers thrust into her hair while she kissed him back with the same burning intensity.

His arms crushed her hard against him, his kiss drowning her until her heart raced against his. His hot mouth moved frenziedly over hers while she twisted her fingers into his thick black hair.

They clung to each other, swaying, and she moaned breathlessly as his hands slid over her tight stomach, moving upwards until they closed over the swell of her breasts and she whimpered, breathless.

'I want you like hell,' he whispered thickly. 'It's eating me up!'

Heat flooded her limbs as he kissed her feverishly, the long fingers shaking as they slid from breast to thigh, his heart crashing hard against his tight chest where she rested her hands.

'Darling,' he groaned against her mouth, and she clung to him in reply, her body winding insidiously against his, her fingers restless as she stroked his neck.

Jacey raised his head, breathing raggedly. He muttered thickly, and closed his eyes, his lashes flickering as he caught his breath.

Louisa swayed against him, pulses drumming in her ears, and watched the fever that made his breathing unsteady, made a muscle jerk in his cheek.

'I've got to have you,' he groaned, his mouth sliding over her throat in burning sensual kisses. 'Tonight—let me love you tonight.'

Thoughts rose drowsily in her mind, and as she waited, they gained credence, gained momentum. She knew Jacey hated her. Whether he wanted to make love to her or not, whether he was hurting himself or not. He hated her, and that hatred would not die in bed. It would only die when he was ready to forgive her. And that wasn't now.

'Say yes,' he muttered against her ear, kissing her lobe, licking it with his tongue until she shivered.

'No, Jacey.'

The silence was deafening. Her cheeks burnt, the blood pulsating in her veins. Then he raised his head, very slowly.

'What did you say?' he asked in a strained, very controlled voice.

Her lower lip trembled as she caught the expression in his eyes. 'I'm sorry,' she whispered.

'Sorry?' His lips curled viciously, and for one moment she thought he might hit her.

She backed, frightened by the violence that leapt from his eyes.

'Sorry,' he bit out, breathing hard, staring at her with incredulous eyes, 'I'll teach you to be sorry! I'll make you wish you'd never been born!'

He turned and slammed out of the kitchen, his shoulders set angrily. As he slammed the door, Louisa jumped, watching the door bang to and fro on its hinges.

She slumped against the wall. The tiles were cold and icy against her skin. Will it never end? she asked herself miserably, and felt a hot tear slide out from beneath her lashes. She wiped it away childishly, her fingers trembling.

CHAPTER SIX

LOUISA didn't want to get out of bed the next morning. Sitting upright, she stared mindlessly at the wall, trying not to think of the wedding ahead of her. Scotty was arriving at eleven to dress at the house with her—but she preferred not to think of that right now. She would get up when he arrived.

But Jacey came to see where she had got to as time went on, and she looked up with a start as the door clicked open and his broad shoulders filled the doorway.

'What,' he asked coolly, 'are you doing? Do you realise what time it is?'

Louisa looked at him steadily. 'Ten-thirty,' she said without looking at the little blue alarm clock beside her. She didn't need to check; she knew perfectly well she should have been up hours ago.

'Out of that bed,' Jacey told her in a warning tone, 'or I'll drag you out!'

She looked at him irritably. 'Just a few more minutes,' she said, snuggling back into the pillow with a sigh. Jacey crossed the room in a flash and his hand closed over her wrist. 'Hey!' she yelped as she tumbled out of bed, almost losing her balance.

'You haven't eaten, and it's getting late,' he told her coolly. 'Go down and get yourself some breakfast.'

'I'll be sick,' she muttered, her face mutinous.

'Good,' he replied, moving to the door. 'It'll put some colour into your cheeks.'

Louisa made a face at his departing back, and picked up her things before going to the bathroom to wash. The hours before the wedding seemed to stretch ahead endlessly. How would she bear it? Waiting for an event like this was worse than actually going through with it!

Scotty arrived dead on time and she made him some coffee, showing him to the room he was to use. He looked around with a bemused expression as he hung his suit up, mumbling something about it being all right for some. Louisa watched him with a smile. He made her feel calm just by being with her.

The long white lace dress rustled at her ankles as Louisa stood in front of the mirror later that day. Her silky black hair was a perfect foil against its delicate white, her large dark eyes peeping out from beneath a flowing veil and small coronet of flowers.

Scotty came in and twirled in front of the mirror, pleased as Punch. 'How do I look?' he asked, adjusting his top hat on his old grey head.

'Very Lord of the Manor,' she said, her cheeks dimpling.

He nodded solemn agreement and turned to study her. 'Beautiful,' he said softly, his eyes moving slowly over her. He stepped forward, picking up a white orchid from the bouquet beside her. 'Here,' he said, putting it in her hair. He smiled. 'The finishing touch.'

Louisa smiled back, but her mouth was taut with strain, and her fingers gripped her bouquet far too tightly.

Scotty sighed. 'It's a proud day for me, leading you up the aisle.' He turned slightly pink, his ears reddening. 'You've been like a daughter to me these last few years,' he said huskily, then frowned. 'But it should be your own father giving you away. It saddens me.'

Louisa looked away, her eyes sad. It saddened her too. She didn't even know who her father was.

Then the car arrived, and they walked to the door, climbing into the white Rolls-Royce and leaving the house empty. The ride to the church played havoc with Louisa's nerves. Her eyes were wide with strain as she looked out of the window, seeing the small white stone church looming up ahead.

A sea of hats bobbed and dipped in the aisle as she walked slowly up it on Scotty's arm. Her heart was pounding as she saw Jacey turn his dark head and their eyes met with a jolt. She was trembling when she reached his side.

'Dearly beloved,' the vicar began, and Louisa glanced nervously at Jacey, her eyes intent on the hard-boned face, the dark lashes which flickered against his tanned skin.

She was intensely aware of Jacey's dark powerful figure as they stood together, saying their vows. Did they mean anything to him? she wondered, watching the hard sensual mouth moving as he spoke.

The cool brush of his fingers on her as he slid the platinum ring on her finger made her tense. Her eyes lifted to his and she saw a flicker of passing emotion in their depths. She wondered again if their vows meant anything to him.

Then they were out in the bright sunshine and Jacey bent his head for the photographers. Louisa trembled as his lips moved sensually over hers, clutching his broad shoulders with white fingers.

Glen and Maggie ran to the car, showering them with rice as they got into the front of it. 'Have fun!' Glen yelled, grinning like a monkey and emptying a box of rice all over Jacey's head.

Jacey started the car and they pulled away. Louisa waved until the crowd was out of sight, then settled back into the seat, feeling more nervous than ever now she was alone again with him.

'Where are we going?' she asked quietly as they sped away from London.

Jacey brushed confetti from his raven-black hair. 'Yorkshire,' he told her shortly.

Her eyes widened. Why Yorkshire? she wondered, frowning. Then she shrugged, and lapsed into silence, watching as they left the urban sprawl of the suburbs behind them, driving on to the motorway where great grassy banks rose up beside them.

Three hours later they pulled up outside a tall grey stone house. The weather had shifted uncertainly all day, but now a storm was in process over the wild sweep of the Yorkshire hills, and thunder vied with lightning for supremacy in the skies.

Greystone House was framed against a tortured sky, the white veins of lightning ripping the sky apart, every crash of thunder making Louisa jump, her eyes darting.

'We'll have to make a run for it,' Jacey said beside her as rain battered the roof of the car. 'This rain drenches!'

She nodded, flicking the door open and dashing head first for the oak door of the house. Although it wasn't far, she was soaked by the time she reached it, and she huddled under the grey slate porch, shivering slightly.

He joined her, his black hair damp, and pushed the door open with the flat of one powerful hand, waiting as she went quickly inside.

He adjusted the collar of his jacket, shaking rain free. His eyes slid over her with amusement. 'You look like a drowned rat,' he commented.

Louisa felt her mouth compress with irritation, but she didn't reply. She followed him along the dark hallway until he pushed open a door and led her inside. It was a large, spacious room, with dark red velvet curtains falling in a single, rippling line to the floor. A grandfather clock ticked sonorously, watching them with its bland round face. Oak panels shone under discreet lighting, the varnish slick against the smooth grain of the wood.

They ate dinner in a tense silence. Louisa felt those silver-green eyes watching her all the time, but when she looked up, Jacey looked away. It was impossible to discover what was going on inside that enigmatic black head.

After dinner she waited until she had finished her coffee, then said, 'I'm rather tired,' and watched him for reaction.

'Tired?' he drawled smokily, then gave her a lazy, barbed smile. 'Then I suggest you splash your face with water. That should wake you up in time.'

In time for what? she thought angrily, going out of the room and up the stairs. Then she realised that she didn't know where her room was. She heard Jacey's footsteps on the stairs and whirled, pulses thudding.

'Lost?'

She nodded, and he stepped forward, opening a door to her left. He made a mocking bow as he watched her step inside. The room was warm and earthy, decorated in dark browns and soft creams, subtly illuminated by gentle lighting.

The door closed behind her and she turned. Jacey leaned lazily against the panel.

Louisa's eyes darted to the bed and she felt them widen with sudden realisation. It was large, dark brown with soft cream pillows on either side. She looked back at Jacey.

'This is my room,' she said, pulses leaping.

He raised one brow. 'Is it?' he drawled softly.

Her heart thrust at her breast. 'There are other rooms.'

He shook his black head. 'I prefer this one.'

Her throat constricted with panic. 'Then I'll sleep elsewhere,' she said, beginning to move towards the door.

Jacey pushed away from the door, wrapped in menace, watching her in silence, his eyes narrowed, pinning her to the spot, while Louisa felt her heart drum furiously as he stood totally still.

She drew an unsteady breath. 'I'm not letting you into my bed, Jacey.'

His smile made her blood run cold. 'Who's Jacey?'

'I won't let you do it.' A frisson of alarm ran through her as she faced him, electricity crackling between them.

His eyes flashed with sudden temper. 'I have no intention of sleeping alone on my wedding night,' he said tightly, then he was coming for her with the tread of a wolf.

Louisa backed, her face whitening. 'And I have no intention of sleeping with you,' she retorted between her teeth, 'so one of us is bound to lose out!'

He stopped, and a slow smile touched his mouth. 'I never lose,' he said softly, and she felt her heart stop for one incredible moment, a shiver running through her as it crashed back into life.

He was closing in on her now, the distance covered quickly by those long muscular legs, and Louisa couldn't take her eyes off him, he looked so intensely sexy.

'I won't let you make love to me,' she said shakily as the long hands came to slide over her shoulders.

'No?' His cool fingertips ran lazily over her neck. 'Any particular reasons?'

She stared at him agitatedly, wanting to tell him why, but not daring to. Her body was in a state of heated excitement mixed with fear and uncertainty. She tried to speak, but nothing came out, until she took a deep breath and plunged in head first.

'Because you hate me!'

There was a little silence, then Jacey drew her closer. 'Hatred is far more exciting in bed,' he drawled, his hard body sliding against hers. 'It becomes more interesting when you add a touch of hate.'

Louisa swallowed, her pulses leaping hotly. 'That isn't making love.'

'Love?' His upper lip curled viciously. 'No such thing, my darling. As you taught me so expertly.'

She caught her breath as the words cut through her, her heart hurting. 'Can't you forget?' she asked angrily, wincing inside. 'Can't you try to understand?'

'Understand?' he said roughly. 'Understand what? That I fell for the same type twice? Went head over heels over a greedy little bitch?' He drew a ragged breath, his face darkening. 'I didn't learn the first time. I had to do it again, all over again.'

Is there no way of reaching him? she thought desperately as she watched him in the silence that followed. He didn't move for a few moments, and she tentatively reached out a trembling hand to touch him.

'Jacey,' she said huskily, her lower lip trembling, 'you're wrong about me.' Her eyes searched his for some sign of emotion other than hate, but she searched in vain.

He gave her a barbed smile. 'Sure—I was wrong about Rachel too, I suppose? I'm wrong about both of you. I just have no judgment when it comes to women.'

She winced at the sniping, angry words clipped from his mouth like bullets. 'Please . . .' she begged, almost in tears, but he broke in without letting her finish, his eyes fierce.

'Please what?' he bit out, breathing hard. 'Please don't upset your ordered little mind by speaking the truth? Too hard to swallow, is it?' His eyes raked her from head to foot with contempt. 'You sicken me,' he told her roughly, eyes burning. 'You've put me through hell, and you don't give a damn. Well, I'll pay you back in your own coin. This marriage is going to burn you up with pain before I'm through!'

He looked at her white, stricken face for a moment, then pushed her away with an effort, turning on his heel to stride out of the room. The door slammed shut behind him, and she jumped, eyes filled with unhappiness.

Tears sprang from her eyes, and she put her hands to her face, drawing a deep, ragged breath. I've gambled and lost, she thought, fighting for control. Jacey hated her far more than he had ever loved her, and when he said he was going to put her through hell, she knew he meant it—every last word.

'How do you fight a wounded animal?' she murmured through her tears, her voice choked.

He was reacting like this because she had hurt him badly. Wounded pride and damaged self-respect were only a small percentage of his anger towards her. His fierce, consuming hatred came from a far deeper wound.

Pulling her clothes off with childlike lack of interest, she heaped them in an untidy pile over the back of a chair. Her case hadn't been brought in from the car, so she had nothing to wear in bed. She slipped naked between the sheets, feeling the tears smudge on the crisp white pillow.

Closing her eyes, she allowed the blanket of sleep to calm her, and memories faded as she slowly fell asleep.

She moaned aloud in her sleep, her dreams filled with a red-hot sensuality that made her naked body twist restlessly as her subconscious gave her everything she needed.

In her mind's eye, she saw the gleam of Jacey's bare skin, his thighs entwined with hers, the brush of his long fingers on her body sending shockwaves of sensual pleasure rippling through her.

Whimpering, she turned her head to his mouth, her lips meeting his in heart-racing passion, the brush of naked skin making her pulses drum frenziedly in her ears.

The dream began to fade, and she tried to catch her breath, her lids lifting limpidly, her skin warm and damp with perspiration, her pulses still drumming like thunder. She didn't want the dream to end, she wanted to go on in that state of unreality where there was no hatred, no anger between them, where love needed no words.

Then she felt long fingers slide sensually to her hips, pulling her seductively against warm, bare skin. Her lids flew open with a gasp.

'No!' she whispered agonisingly. Jacey lay beneath her. She couldn't speak, couldn't move. She just stared down at him, her body rigid.

'You're not going to stop me,' he whispered, looking at her through half-closed lids, perspiration dewing his dark lashes, his mouth parted with breathless desire.

Louisa tried to speak, but couldn't. Her heart was hurting as it hammered fast against her chest with desire and shock. She could feel him beneath her, aware in every nerve of his lean, hard-muscled body.

She tried to raise herself up. His eyes fell to her naked breasts and she heard his harsh intake of breath.

'Yes . . .' he muttered thickly.

Then he moved, turning her over, lying on top of her while she struggled breathlessly, her hands thrusting into his thick dark hair, her body bucking and writhing beneath him.

'Don't fight me . . .' he whispered hoarsely, his

hands sliding inexorably to her thighs. 'Don't fight me, please . . .'

He drove into her in one exquisite movement and she whimpered with the unbearable ecstasy, her hands softening, sliding to cling to his back, caught up in the frenzied lack of inhibition which had been in her dream.

Her hands were in his hair, sliding feverishly along his naked spine, his hips, while she moaned, every thought driven out of her mind inexorably except one, I love you I love you don't stop, she could hear the hoarse, agonised note of his voice as he whispered her name, his ragged breathing, the rapid harsh thud of his heart against her own, I love you I love you don't stop, and the tension coiled tight inside her, growing until she couldn't breathe, her chest constricted, eyes tightly shut, mouth parted wide in gasping ecstasy as she clung to him, don't stop don't stop, then it snapped and she drove against him in dizzying rapid movements, teeth clenched, sweat dripping from her body, breath forced from her in gasps as she heard his hoarse voice crying her name above her, his fingers biting into her flesh while she shuddered with convulsive pleasure beneath him.

The fever subsided. Louisa lay limp and drained, resting her hands on his damp back, needing to feel some sort of physical contact after the storm of emotion which had been in their lovemaking.

She rested her hand on his neck, feeling the damp strands of hair beneath her fingertips, the warm pulse that drummed throughout his body.

Jacey looked so vulnerable; his face was relaxed,

his eyes closed. The long dark lashes rested sleepily on his tanned cheek, dewed with perspiration. Louisa looked at his face and felt her heart wrench with a sigh. All the hatred, all the anger, was smoothed out, leaving a calm handsome friend in her arms instead of a bitter enemy.

Running her fingers along his warm naked spine, she smiled secretly to herself. It was so good to see him like this. Welcome back, she thought, her eyes closing.

Then Jacey raised his head to look down at her. 'Was it good, my darling?' he murmured, but something in his voice made her eyes open with unease.

A smile flickered on her mouth. 'You know it was,' she said huskily, and tensed as she saw the warning light in his eyes.

'Better than Radcliffe?'

She closed her eyes. 'Jacey, please——'

'Or did he have a different technique?'

Her mouth tightened. 'Stop it, Jacey!'

His smile was cruel. 'You must tell me. I know how much you like variety—I wouldn't want you to get bored.'

'How can you say that?' she said through white lips, her eyes flashing angrily.

'Easy,' he gritted through his teeth, 'I just open my mouth and the words come out.'

Louisa stared at him bitterly. 'Damn you! What do you want from me?'

His eyes were stormy as he stared down at her, holding her upright. 'I want to watch you suffer,' he said under his breath. 'I want to watch you go through the same hell you put me through.'

Shock made her heart stop beating for one

terrifying moment as she heard his words, felt them sink in, hurting her, while she just stared at him in blinding disbelief.

Then she started to shake with rage, her face white. 'If you hate me so much, why did you marry me?'

'*Hate you?*' As if compelled, his hands came down and held her head tightly, shaking it slightly, angrily. 'I loved you!' he said hoarsely, holding her like a rag doll. 'And you betrayed me. You took everything I had and then you kicked my teeth in.'

'No,' she moaned, shaking her head, her eyes blurring, 'I thought you'd gone. I thought you'd left me!'

'Liar! You might have fooled Radcliffe but you'll never fool me!'

Through the haze of tears she saw his violently angry face, saw the rage of emotion in his eyes. A sob choked her throat and she flinched away from him, her hands trembling.

'Do you know what it feels like?' he asked raggedly. 'I'll tell you. It feels like having your guts kicked out.'

'Don't . . .' she moaned, tears coursing hotly over her cheeks.

'And you'll feel it Louisa,' he said, breathing hoarsely. 'You're going to go through everything I went through. I'm going to settle the score between us.'

He pushed her away roughly, standing up and dressing quickly. Louisa watched him through a haze of tears and bitter self-reproach, cursing herself for the day she let her pride smash everything they had had. It was all doubling back on her now. She would have been able to face it if he had given her a guarantee that at the end of it all he would love her again, hold her without hurting her. But how could he do that? His hatred might never die, and the realisation was like a nail driven through her heart.

He was buttoning the smooth black waistcoat, looking at her without feeling, and she made one last desperate attempt to reach him.

'Jacey...!' She held out her hand, eyes pleading.

But he was gone.

Jacey drove to the village in the afternoon, leaving Louisa alone in the house, giving her too much time to think. She sat in the elegant drawing room feeling a grey cloud of depression pressing down on her.

Among his records, she had found a Julio Iglesias L.P. and slipped it on the turntable, closing her eyes wearily. The yearning emotion in the song made her heart miss a beat, the dark velvety voice of the singer touching something deep inside her as she listened, empathising with the feeling in the song.

The door opened, but she didn't hear it because she was too wrapped up in her thoughts and the stirring lyric of the song. Jacey stood watching her in silence for a moment.

She looked up as the music ended and her eyes widened in surprise. 'Hallo,' she said nervously, studying him, her gaze intent.

He watched her, unsmiling, his body still. Then he moved to the stereo and switched the record off. 'We're going out tonight,' he told her curtly.

'Oh?' She sat up, embarrassed because he'd seen her unguarded face for a few seconds while she was involved with her thoughts and emotions. 'Where?'

'Some friends of mine live next door.' He slipped the record back in its cover, glancing at the dark-haired man on the front before putting it away. 'Wear something sexy, but not formal.'

It was almost a command. 'Yes, Jacey,' she said through pale lips, her eyes angry.

His gaze flicked to her. 'Obedience,' he drawled, his mouth crooking sardonically. 'It warms my heart.'

Louisa watched as he went out of the room, then slumped back in the chair sighing. It was impossible.

At seven-thirty, she stood in the hall waiting, wearing a pale blue dress that flared at the hips with a low neckline discreetly showing the gold medallion that nestled between her breasts. A scent of perfume hovered around her.

Jacey joined her in the hall looking sexy in black trousers, smartly casual hacking jacket and a white open-necked shirt. Louisa looked at his brown throat and felt her mouth go dry.

'In front of Elizabeth and Rizzio,' he said coldly, 'you will behave yourself. I don't want them to think this is anything but a love match.'

Her lips tightened. 'Yes, Jacey,' she muttered.

His face tightened for a moment, then he took her hand, hustling her out of the door and into the garden. The storm had died down overnight, and the late evening sunshine warmed her face. The path was smeared with mud from yesterday's rain, the grass still damp beneath her feet.

Elizabeth and Rizzio's house was a rambling old family house. The garden was wild and overgrown with thorns and bushes and thistles sprouting in mad abandon. Red stone walls were busily being invaded by sneaky plants that crept across to windows which were peeling with age.

The door opened and a huge black dog lolloped out. 'Basil!' yelled a voice. The dog bounded on to Jacey, eyes rolling, tail thumping and wagging as it howled ecstatically and licked Jacey with a long pink tongue.

A small rather scatty woman came after it. 'Naughty Basil!' she reprimanded, yanking it back. 'No dinner for you!'

Basil howled piteously and rolled his eyes.

'Hallo, Elizabeth,' Jacey smiled, kissing her powdered cheek. 'I see Basil's still in need of a good trainer.'

Elizabeth frowned. She looked like her garden—her hair sprouting in brown abandon, her clothes heaped together in a madcap way, her beady blue eyes the colour of delphiniums.

'Hallo,' she offered Louisa her hand. 'We met at the wedding. You remember me—I had my flower show hat on.'

'Of course!' said Louisa as a vivid image of a walking flower shop came into her head. How could she forget?

'Come in,' Elizabeth said briskly. 'Rizzio will get you a drink while I see to Basil Baskerville.'

Louisa's eyes met Jacey's. 'Basil Baskerville?' she whispered, laughing.

He tapped his head with one long finger. 'They're both as mad as hatters,' he murmured conspiratorially.

They went into the hall, which was a jumble of old magazines, pieces of paper and a collection of worn out shoes heaped in a corner by the telephone table, and followed Elizabeth into the main room of the house.

'Hallo!' A lanky energetic man with rippling black curls and a hollow face greeted them. He came over to them, one bony hand outstretched, a melon-like grin on his face.

'Good to see you, Rizzio,' said Jacey, shaking his hand.

'You too, Jason. I loved the wedding—all that free food and drink!' Rizzio laughed, eyes twinkling.

Elizabeth came in behind them with a grimace. 'I hate weddings. I see all my old friends and relatives and think—Don't they look old?' She gave Louisa a wry smile. 'Then I stay away from mirrors until the shock wears off!'

'Dreadful weather last night, wasn't it?' Rizzio went over to a drinks cabinet in the corner and began unscrewing bottles. 'All that thunder and lightning belonged more in a Dracula movie. I kept expecting Bela Lugosi to leap out of the undergrowth baring his fangs!'

Louisa laughed, and went to sit down in a chair. The room was a complete mess. The piano was covered in dirty old newspapers, a table nearby stacked with record covers. Ashtrays overflowed from corner to corner, old wine glasses stuck to the mantelpiece.

'Here,' Rizzio came over with a tall glass filled with green liquid, 'a Rizzio Special. I bet you'll love it.'

It looked like a fruit shop. She sipped it and

grimaced. 'You'd lose the bet,' she said drily, eyeing it. It was utterly poisonous. An assortment of fruit was stuck to the rim with a little paper umbrella attached. Typical that it should be green, though, she thought, looking at Rizzio—he reminded her of Captain Hook, and he was notorious for his poisoned green cakes.

Jacey perched on the arm of her chair, his long legs resting next to her fingers. Louisa looked at his lean flat stomach and felt her mouth go dry. She turned away, her lashes sweeping her cheeks.

Elizabeth came over with a tray of biscuits, and offered them round. 'I baked them this afternoon,' she said, eyeing them dubiously, 'but something went wrong. I hate baking—I don't know why I bother.'

Louisa picked up an unfortunate gingerbread man who had been deprived of one arm and bit into his misshapen head. Jacey demurred with a charming smile, but Basil wasn't so choosy. He crept in and slid his long black nose up to the plate.

'Don't you dare!' Elizabeth said irritably, grabbing at his collar.

Basil gave her a naughty look and pinched a biscuit. He dodged a smack and slid off into a corner, wagging his tail.

'I enjoyed the wedding,' said Rizzio, leaning against the piano, 'but why hadn't we seen you before? Were you Top Secret?'

There was a little silence.

Jacey glanced at Louisa, eyes hooded. 'I kept her under lock and key,' he explained, and Louisa's eyes narrowed. There was more truth in that than the others would realise, she thought bitterly.

'Why didn't we see any of your family there?' Rizzio asked, his head tilted. He rootled around in an old box, fishing out a box of matches and lighting a French cigarette. 'It looked odd—your side of the church was empty.'

She looked away. 'I haven't got any family,' she said huskily, but her eyes met Jacey's, and the expression in them made her heart miss a beat. Did he know something? He was watching her coolly, eyes narrowed. Louisa bit her lower lip anxiously.

Elizabeth was appalled. 'Oh, how terrible for you!' she said, her lips disappearing with disapproval. 'I don't know what I'd do without my family.'

'Cheer?' Rizzio suggested wickedly.

She gave him an offended look. 'At least my family are sane—more than can be said for yours! They're a bunch of raving lunatics—especially your Uncle Willy.'

Jacey touched Louisa's hand with long cool fingers. 'Poor darling,' he murmured, eyes meeting hers. She held her breath for a split second. There was something in his face that made her think he knew something. Or was it just her imagination?

Elizabeth served dinner at eight. She had attempted a curry which had gone disastrously wrong, and everyone sat around the table staring at it with polite smiles. Elizabeth was not to be misled, however. She doled out curdled curry sauce to everyone, glaring at them, daring them to mention how awful it looked.

After dinner they all sat around the room drinking coffee among the higgledy-piggledy piles of magazines and newspapers. Jacey slid his arm around Louisa, and she looked up at him, seeing the calculating light in his eyes. She frowned, not daring to push him away as he muzzled her throat with cool lips. He would only be angry with her if she did.

The heavy thud of his heart beneath her hands made her own pulses leap in response. She felt every hair on the back of her neck prickling with awareness, and was glad when they finally left the house.

'Why did you do that?' she asked as they let themselves into the house. 'Keep kissing me like that in front of them?'

He eyed her silently, reaching out a hand to flick on the hall light. 'They expect a honeymoon couple to want to spend all their time in bed.' He ran a finger slowly over her neck. 'And we are a honeymoon couple.'

Her smile was tight. 'But we don't want to spend all our time in bed.'

Jacey's eyes glittered. 'Don't we?' he murmured.

Louisa drew an unsteady breath and began to move past him. But Jacey moved quickly, his hand shooting out to grip her arm, whipping her against his lean hard body, his fingers sliding to span her slender waist.

'Where do you think you're going?' he drawled against her ear.

'To bed,' she said stiffly, adding in a cold voice, 'Alone.'

His fingers slid very slowly to her hips, pulling her harder against him, his lean body pressed against hers, his legs brushing the top of her thighs as his mouth touched her throat.

'Not alone,' he said deeply, 'not ever again. You're my wife now.'

Her pulses leapt as his lips brushed her skin. 'Last night was enough for me,' she said tautly. 'I don't want you again.'

He stiffened, standing deathly still. The air was suddenly fraught with tension. Louisa heard the thud of her heart in the tense silence, and began to tremble against his still unmoving body.

'What did you say?' he muttered thickly.

She drew an unsteady breath. 'I don't want you, Jacey,' she whispered.

His hands clamped on her shoulders, whirling her to face him. 'I don't give a damn what you want,' he said roughly. He bent his head to kiss her, but she pushed him away, hard.

'No!' she exclaimed fiercely, trying to get away, and his eyes flashed with sudden anger.

'Don't push me away, you little bitch!' he bit out, and one hand thrust into her hair, jerking her head painfully backwards, his nails raking her scalp while his hot mouth descended on hers, kissing her ruthlessly, making her heart hammer inside her as she desperately pushed at his chest.

Jerking her head away suddenly, she stared at him, breathing fast. 'This isn't a marriage!' she said bitterly. 'This is legalised prostitution. You think you can have me whenever you want.'

'I'm glad you understand me,' he said through his teeth. 'Don't you find it more exciting to be a whore instead of a wife?'

Her eyes flashed. 'You bastard,' she whispered, and her hand stung viciously across his face, her fingers hurting from the force of the blow. His head jerked back in incredulous rage, eyes blazing as he looked down at her, jaw clamped.

'Wrong person,' he bit out. 'I thought you were the bastard.'

Her heart stopped beating, all the breath knocked out of her as though he'd punched her. She felt shattered, incredulous, staring at him with painful disbelief, her face draining of all colour until she was white as chalk. She stared at him in total shattered silence for what seemed centuries.

Jacey drew a ragged breath. 'That was uncalled for. I'm sorry.'

Louisa was speechless. Who could have told him? Scotty? Her heart hurt. No, Scotty would never have betrayed her, would never have told anyone without her permission. But no one else knew, she thought frantically, no one else knew.

She forced herself to speak, her words jerky and tight. 'How did you find out?'

'Does it matter?' he asked grimly.

Anger flared in her eyes. 'Of course it matters!' she said bitterly. She had thought she was safe, had thought she had left it in her past, locked behind her. But now Jacey had sprung the lock and the secret was out, reverberating through her mind like a bullet.

'Look,' Jacey gave a harsh sigh, a red stain running along his cheek, 'I'm sorry. Can't we forget I ever said it? If I'd been in my right mind I would never have mentioned it '

'Forget? Forget?' she echoed frantically, eyes burning into his. 'Oh, Jacey, how could you say it? How *could* you?' Her eyes closed with pain, and she shook her head. 'I knew you hated me, but I didn't realise quite how much

He pushed his hands into his pockets, muttering impatiently under his breath. 'I wasn't trying to hurt you,' he said roughly. 'I was angry, I lost my head.' He spread his hands in front of him. 'I don't see why it upsets you so much.'

'No,' she said angrily, 'you wouldn't You haven't had to live with it. Love child, that's what they used to call me.' Her mouth twisted. 'And that's when they were being kind. Usually they were more brutal.'

She shuddered, twisting her mind from the unkind memories that threatened to make her lose control. She had wanted to tell Jacey so many times before, but something had always held her back. She had been too scared of rejection to risk telling him.

'How did you find out?' she asked, looking back at him.

He shifted, shrugging. 'Lucky guess?'

'Try again,' she said tightly. 'Did you ask Scotty? Is that how you know? Or did you send one of your loyal henchmen on a crusade?'

He watched her grimly for a long moment. There was a peculiar stillness between them.

'Louisa,' he said slowly, 'I don't care that you're illegitimate . . .'

'Don't say that word!' Her hands flew to cover her ears, blocking out the awful sound of the word which had haunted her for so long. She couldn't bear to hear it ringing from corner to corner.

He lost his temper. 'For God's sake!' he said bitingly. 'It can't be that bad.'

'How do you know?' she flared, her body shaking with sudden rage. 'You had no right to delve into my past like that. You should never have damned well interfered!'

He reached out impatiently for her. 'Louisa——!' he began angrily.

'Get out of my sight!' she broke in, pushing him away, bitterness flaring from the tormented black eyes. They stared at each other for a long moment, conflict raging between them.

His hand dropped to his side. 'I'll wait for you upstairs,' he said tightly, thrusting his hands into the pockets of his trousers and turning to walk up the stairs to their bedroom.

She glared after him. 'You'll wait for ever!'

Louisa walked into the kitchen, reaching out one hand to the cupboard and picking up a plate. Aiming it at the wall, she flung it and it smashed noisily, splintering into dozens of small pieces that showered in an arc across the kitchen. The crash hurt her ears, but it satisfied her.

Hot tears streamed down her cheeks, running into her mouth as she reached with one trembling hand for another plate. She hurled it at the wall, taking her anger out on the china with deep satisfaction.

The pieces of china danced across the smooth brown linoleum at her feet, fragments of it nipping her ankles, the sharp pain getting through to the core of her anger, calming her.

'Damn you, Jacey,' she whispered bitterly, and hurled another plate, tears burning her eyes.

CHAPTER SEVEN

ELIZABETH called round the next morning just as Louisa had finished dressing and was coming down the stairs. She went to the door with a frown, wondering who it was, and was surprised to see her standing on the doorstep. Jacey's footsteps were heard as he came down the stairs behind her.

'Who is it?' he asked, coming down the hall, and Louisa opened the door wider so that he could see. 'God help us,' he muttered, smiling wryly as he saw Elizabeth. 'You haven't got that wretched hound with you, I hope?'

Elizabeth shook her head. 'He's eating Rizzio's slippers. I decided not to disturb him.'

'In that case,' said Jacey, 'you can come in.' He picked up his paper from the hall table where Louisa had put it and wandered into the living room, flicking it out with a rustle as he started to read while he walked.

Elizabeth wiped her feet on the front door mat. 'I popped round on the offchance that you'd be going into York today,' she said, eyeing Louisa with beady eyes. 'Are you?'

Louisa shrugged. 'Who knows?' She smiled, closing the door, and they went into the living room to sit with Jacey. 'Why? Did you want a lift?'

Jacey lowered his paper and she met his long cool appraisal, feeling a shiver run through her. Whenever he looked at her she felt the same heart-stopping emotion. Can't he see that? she asked herself, frowning. Or is he blind? She sighed—no doubt he thought she was feeling self-pity, not love.

'I think we can manage that,' Jacey drawled, folding his paper and putting it down. 'Is it just shopping you wanted to do?'

Elizabeth ran a hand over her madcap curls. 'Just bits and pieces,' she said, giving him a little smile. 'You know, a couple of bottles of arsenic for Rizzio and so on.'

He laughed, then turned those devastating eyes on Louisa for a moment. 'Go and get ready, darling,' he said huskily. 'We'll leave in a few minutes.'

She nodded, flushing at the tender note in his voice. Was that really just there for Elizabeth's benefit? Or did he still feel something, *anything*, for her?

They left the house ten minutes later, driving swiftly across the ragged Yorkshire countryside, and arrived in York at eleven. Elizabeth wandered off on her own arranging to meet them both in an hour outside the Minster on the small green there.

Jacey took her into a small coffee house after they had walked around the town, and they sat at a small gingham-covered table on wooden chairs while the noise of people talking and cups clinking went on around them.

'Enjoy yourself last night?' The cool dark voice made her jump, droplets of hot coffee hitting her hand.

'Yes,' she said, recovering, 'they were very lively.'

'I meant the little plate-smashing episode,' he told her drily. 'You sounded as though you were having a lovely time. Were you?'

'Yes, thank you,' said Louisa, looking obstinate. 'I haven't had so much fun in years.'

He held her eyes for a long silent moment. Then, 'I'm sorry,' he said deeply.

She couldn't believe her ears, staring at him amazed. 'What?'

'About last night.' He looked down at the red and white check gingham tablecloth. 'I didn't realise it would hurt you so much. It wasn't intentional.'

Their eyes met again, and Louisa's heart skidded crazily. 'It's been said before,' she told him huskily. 'You learn to live with it. It's just that particular word that gets to me.'

He watched her intently. 'I can imagine.'

She bent her head. It was a thorn in her flesh which had never been wholly removed. People had to learn to live with things which were often unpalatable, unacceptable. She had tried so many times to convince herself that her illegitimacy didn't exist, tried to pretend she was like everyone else.

But it was a part of her. It was something which would always be there, however hard she tried to ignore it, however much she was afraid of it hurting her.

Last night she had learnt, finally, that it didn't matter that she was illegitimate. It didn't matter to Jacey and it didn't matter to her. It had been the shock of hearing it from his lips that had driven her into a rage. Now that it was out in the open between them she would feel much easier about it. It was no longer a secret, no longer a fear.

How many times, she wondered, had she been scared of rejection because of it? She'd been afraid that Jacey would reject her if he had found out.

But now she realised that if he had, he wouldn't have been worth keeping at all.

Louisa had often felt like a baby lamb, branded at birth—however old she grew, however deep her thoughts became, she had felt that the brand would remain in her flesh, a constant reminder of the legacy of her birth.

But it was all a question of acceptance. Okay, she was illegitimate—so what? Who cared? Anyone who thought less of her could go to hell.

Once it was accepted, it would be put behind her, forgotten. It would always be there, always be a truth, a part of her. But it couldn't hurt her. Not ever again.

'Why didn't you tell me?' Jacey asked, head tilted. 'I thought I knew everything about you.'

'I was scared,' she admitted huskily.

The black brows jerked together. 'Scared? Did you think it would change my mind about you?'

She nodded, studying him thoughtfully.

'You must be crazy!' He stared at her, the green eyes dazzling with the rays of sunlight reflecting off the irises. 'Either that or you have a pretty low opinion of me.'

'Or maybe I've come up against that kind of thinking before,' she pointed out softly.

He ran a hand through his thick black hair. 'Some people can be pretty brutal,' he said with feeling. 'But me? Surely you know me well enough to know it wouldn't make a shred of difference?'

She laughed at that, leaning back in her seat and looking at him wryly. 'Now who's being crazy?'

He frowned, his eyes narrowing. 'Okay,' he said under his breath, 'I'll admit you didn't know enough about me. But you knew *me*, the kind of man I am.'

Her brows rose and she sighed. 'That's like a house without furniture. I knew your first name, your phoney address and your age. What else did I know?' She spread her hands, shaking her head. 'Nothing.'

'Be reasonable,' he muttered. 'What would you have done if I'd told you? I can just picture it— "Hey, Louisa, I forgot to mention it, but I'm married to another woman." ' He broke off, watching her. 'You would have hit the roof.'

They watched each other in a brooding silence, and Louisa felt herself sigh irritably. He still wouldn't agree that his secrecy had destroyed them more than any other factor.

'Can we get off this subject?' she asked shortly. 'I've really had enough of the past to last me a lifetime. It's like living with a corpse.'

Jacey stopped dead, his face tightening as he looked at her. 'The past is what brought us here,' he reminded her through thin lips.

'Yes,' she said under her breath, 'and it's destroying our marriage too.' She put her cup down with a crash and several other customers turned to stare, 'Is that what you want? Is that what you really want, Jacey?'

He watched her intently, eyes narrowed. 'Damn you,' he muttered tightly, 'everything that happened to us was your fault.'

Louisa closed her eyes. 'Oh, you idiot!' she exclaimed under her breath, and stood up to leave, feeling bitter anger rise inside her, unable to look at him any more.

His hand shot out to grip her wrist. 'Sit down!'

he ordered through his teeth, and she was so startled by the tone of his voice that she stared at him, sitting back down slowly.

There was a peculiar stillness between them as they watched each other across the small table. Then Jacey ran a hand through his rich dark hair with a harsh sigh.

'I don't like this any more than you do,' he said coldly, his mouth a harsh line. 'Do you think I enjoy living like this?'

Louisa searched his eyes and leaned forward with a sigh. 'Then why keep it up?' she asked gently. 'Can't you try to put it behind you? We'll never make it if you don't.'

The dark lashes flickered as he looked directly at her. 'It's not quite so simple,' he said roughly. 'You've got me so tangled up I don't know what I feel any more.' He stood up abruptly, pushing his chair back with one hand and thrusting some notes on the table before walking out of the little café. Louisa flushed under the curious gazes of the other customers, then stood up with a sigh, following Jacey out into the street.

That evening they went to a nightclub in York. Louisa was glad of the respite. Jacey had been impossible all afternoon, and although he had livened up when Elizabeth and Rizzio had suggested going to the nightclub, he had remained brooding most of the time. Louisa didn't think she could take the hostility between Jacey and herself.

It was like living on top of a minefield. Every step she took was edged with danger—she never knew whether Jacey would explode, devastating her completely.

Elizabeth and Rizzio had spent the afternoon scouring the village looking for someone to babysit their dog for the evening.

'I'll never be able to face the Vicar again!' Elizabeth complained as they ate their dinner in the dark nightclub. 'Basil will probably eat him out of house and vestry.'

'Poor Basil,' said Rizzio, frowning, 'he'd be heartbroken to hear you.'

'I still say we should have locked him in the potting shed,' Elizabeth muttered irritably, spooning the last of her sherry trifle around the bowl without interest.

The nightclub was small and lively, with bright lights around the stage and bouncy music piped through speakers. Mirrors dazzled from wall to wall, nubile young cocktail waitresses wandered around dressed in short black lace dresses and vacant expressions.

'Did you see Maggie at the wedding?' Rizzio asked with an eager expression. 'Didn't she look awful? And just imagine—she's married to someone, poor swine. That hat she was wearing! It was like half of London Zoo on her head.'

Elizabeth laughed, looking at Louisa drily. 'He's a real bitch, isn't he?' she said with amusement.

Jacey was watching with a lazy smile. 'He can't help himself, Elizabeth,' he drawled, holding a cigar between sinewy fingers. 'He's an eccentric genius—you should know that by now.'

Rizzio pretended amazement. 'Eccentric? Me?'

Elizabeth gave him a wry look. 'Listen, kiddo, if you had a belfry, there'd be bats in it!'

Louisa laughed, watching them. Then her gaze fell on Jacey and she felt a sigh escape her throat.

He was relaxed, his lean body at ease, and she urgently wanted to twine her fingers with his across the table in the same easy way she had once been able to do when they were out together. But that had all finished a long time ago, she thought sadly. If only she had had more foresight and a little less pride!

'How did you find this place?' Jacey asked, drawing on his cigar. 'I've never heard of it before.'

'My nephew works behind the bar,' Rizzio told him, waving long fingers in the direction of the bar.

'His family are like ferrets,' said Elizabeth, sighing. 'Everywhere we go they seem to pop out of the woodwork. I wish I'd married an orphan!'

Jacey looked at Louisa grimly, and she flushed, looking away.

'My nephew said the group is ace,' Rizzio continued, scratching his head with bony fingers. 'It's a new group, called Boulevard.'

'Boulevard!' Louisa could hardly believe her ears. That was Pete's group! What on earth are they doing in York? she thought anxiously.

Across the table, her eyes met Jacey's, and the grim set of his face made her heart plummet. He knew it was Pete's group.

She looked up just then as the group came on stage. The sound of clicking microphones filled the club as they adjusted the stands, the rap of drums was heard as Steve began tapping out preparatory rhythms. Then they began to play a current hit from the charts.

Pete was singing into the microphone, his guitar swinging at his hips as he played. Louisa ran her eyes over the rest of the group, taking in the smart appearance of them under the white moon of the spotlight.

'We'll dance,' Jacey drawled as they began to play slow numbers later on the programme.

Louisa stood up, her legs shaky, her eyes riveted on Jacey. His lean hand slid around her waist as he led her to the dance floor, sliding his arms around her and drawing her closer.

Pete faltered on a line as he caught sight of them dancing.

'I think he's jealous,' Jacey murmured in her ear, his fingers sliding through the silkiness of her hair. 'Don't you?'

Louisa shivered as she felt his hard thighs brushing sensuously against hers. 'No. He's probably just surprised,' she said, her voice shaky.

The long hands moved down to her waist. 'Then we must make him jealous, mustn't we, my darling?' he drawled against her throat, his mouth burning on her white skin.

The drugging sensuality of the dance made her cling to him like a limpet, her arms wound around his neck, her fingers tangling in his hair. Their thighs intertwined, their bodies moving together like serpents, sliding against each other with sensual, heated but discreet movements.

The music stopped and she swayed against him, dizzy, her cheeks hot with arousal. Jacey looked down at her through heavy lids, his narrowed gaze inspecting her flushed face.

The group had come to the end of their short programme, and the applause rang out in the small club. Pete and the rest of the band walked off stage.

'I think we upset your wealthy friend,' Jacey drawled, his mouth indenting sardonically.

Louisa looked at him, her mind clearing. 'How can you be so cruel?' she asked, her brow marred with a frown. Pete must have been very upset when he saw them. No doubt he had thought he would be able to escape once he was out of London.

Jacey smiled, his teeth white and sharp. 'I'm just a responsive pupil,' he said with a trace of anger. 'You taught me how to hurt. You can hardly blame me for trying out my skills.'

Her mouth tightened at his words, her eyes angry. 'Sometimes,' she said in a low voice, 'I really dislike you, Jacey.'

His teeth met. 'The feeling is mutual,' he said tightly.

She pushed away from him, walking out of the club and into the foyer. What was the point in arguing with him? He had seen how white Pete had gone when he saw them together, he had seen the anguish in his eyes. How could he have been so deliberately cruel? To hurt someone like that. It just didn't add up to the Jacey she had fallen in love with.

The foyer was cool, the air blowing through the open glass doors, cooling her hot cheeks. She sighed, leaning against the wall, closing her eyes.

'Hey, Louisa!' A familiar voice made her look up, and she saw Steve, the drummer, approaching her. 'How are you doing?'

She straightened, giving him a little smile. 'Hallo, Steve. I'm fine. And you?'

'Fine,' he replied. 'How'd you like the new gear?' He twirled, hand on hip, showing off his new outfit. 'Really cool, huh?'

Her cheeks dimpled as she watched him. 'Really cool,' she agreed, eyeing the smooth line of black jeans and white shirt.

Steven hooted, parading about, cheeks sucked in. 'I feel weird looking nice,' he told her, grinning through his beard. 'I'm so used to everyone calling me Pig-Pen!'

Louisa laughed, her eyes dancing. Then she saw Pete. He stood watching her, his face white, his eyes holding a sadness that made her wince. She bit her lip, uncertain whether she should stay or go. Did he want to even speak to her after what had happened?

Pete walked over to her, his expression unassuming. 'Hallo,' he said quietly. She didn't know how to reply, just gave him a choked smile. He studied her. 'How's marriage?'

She tried to smile, but went wrong halfway. 'Not too bad,' she said huskily, avoiding his eyes for a moment. Searching for something to say, she added, 'I liked the group—you've improved.'

Pete shrugged. 'Yeah, we put some new numbers in the act.' He paused, watching her. 'Come backstage and say hello to the boys. They'll be pleased to see you. You know, they're always asking after you.'

Her eyes darted to the club. Would Jacey miss her if she was gone a little too long? She shrugged, sighing. By the time he thought something might be wrong she would have returned. Besides, he had made her angry, and she wasn't prepared to go back to that hostility yet.

She hesitated. 'Can we walk instead?' she asked softly.

Pete nodded. 'Sure.' He took her arm, leading

her away, and she looked round to say goodbye to Steve, but he had already gone. They walked out of the club together and into the dark street, the lights from the nearby shops softening the darkness.

'How's he treating you?' Pete asked into the silence.

The cool wind blew a strand of hair into her eyes and she smoothed it back absently. 'Fine,' she said with a little smile.

Pete studied her intently, his eyes concerned. 'He seemed like a pretty violent guy when I met him. I wouldn't want to think of him hurting you, Louisa.'

She looked at him through her lashes. 'Jacey wouldn't hurt me,' she said huskily, and it *wasn't* a lie. Jacey became violent only because his emotions ran so deeply. In her book, that didn't constitute hurting.

Time passed while she walked along the streets of York with Pete, and she didn't notice how quickly it had flitted past. There was something peaceful about the empty streets, the cool silence that surrounded the darkness.

'We'd better get back,' said Pete, glancing at his watch. 'It'll be closing time soon.'

'Closing time?' She was horrified, her eyes widening. 'We must hurry. He'll kill me if I'm not back in time!'

She felt her pulses leaping with sudden fear as they ran quickly back along the way they had come, past half-lit shops, past empty roads, uselessly changing traffic lights with no cars to stop at them.

The foyer was jam-packed with people when

they arrived. They were leaving, dragging their coats behind them as they spilled out on to the pavement in a lively jumble of glittering clothes and laughter. Louisa searched their flushed happy faces for Jacey, but he was nowhere to be seen.

Pushing through the club, she looked frantically inside the main part, but she could see neither Jacey, Elizabeth or Rizzio, and her heart gave a painful heavy thud as she stared in disbelief at their deserted table.

'I'll explain what happened,' said Pete with concern as he took her arm and led her outside.

Louisa closed her eyes. 'Don't do that,' she pleaded, breathing hectically at the very idea. 'Please—don't do that!'

They raced to the back of the club, and Louisa's eyes darted around in search of Jacey's car among the lines of cars in the car park. But it wasn't there.

'Hi!' Steve waved to them from the back of a bright orange van with the message 'Boulevard Rules O.K.' painted on it in blue letters. 'I thought you'd gone. What brings you back, then?'

Louisa stopped dead. Slowly she walked over to Steve, eyes worried, 'What do you mean, you thought we'd gone?'

Steve shrugged. 'Your husband was here looking for you about twenty minutes ago. I told him you'd gone.'

Louisa whitened, swaying. She put out a hand to steady herself.

'You bloody idiot!' Pete snapped. 'Why the hell did you tell him that?'

Steve pulled a face. 'I didn't know you hadn't

gone.' He looked at them both, frowning. 'Sorry. Have I put my foot in it?'

Pete ran a weary hand over his forehead. He turned to Louisa. 'You'll have to come back to the hotel with us. You can ring him from there.'

Steve jumped into the front of the van, scratching his head and looking innocent. Louisa found herself squashed between him and Pete as they rode to the hotel, the van rattling noisily as they bumped about, the instruments and other members of the group in the back of the van jumping and rattling as they drove.

She and Pete spent long agonising minutes in the hotel foyer poring over the telephone directories in the plastic-covered telephone booth in the corner of the foyer.

'He's not there,' Louisa announced miserably, snapping the book shut after looking in it a final time.

Pete's thin brows jerked in a frown. 'Let me have a look.' He took the directory, leaning against the coin box, studying the columns with a frown. 'You're right,' he said eventually, putting the book back with disgust.

Louisa studied her watch. Two in the morning. The watch face stared back at her as panic inside her grew. Jacey would hit the roof!

'Taxis,' said Pete after a moment's thought. 'We might find a firm who'll agree to spend hours driving around the countryside looking for the house.'

An hour later, they found a service who agreed finally to send a driver. Pete led her out of the hotel when the green mini-cab pulled up.

'Daylight robbery,' he muttered. 'Charging three times the price just because it's after midnight!

Even in London they're not that bad.'

Louisa looked up at him gratefully. 'Thanks for your help, Pete.'

He smiled. 'Idiot! You wouldn't be in this mess if it hadn't been for me.' He frowned. 'I still think I should have driven you home, though.'

'*Not* a very good idea,' Louisa replied, shivering at the thought of pulling up outside in Pete's car while Jacey watched from a window. 'Besides, you would have got lost on the way back.'

Pete watched her for a long moment as the taxi's engine hummed beside them. He slid his arms hesitantly around her, holding her close, his mouth against her hair.

'I still care about you,' he murmured against her hair, his hand tight on her shoulders. 'You know that. Any time you need me, just let me know. I'll always be around.'

Louisa felt guilt pressing down on her. 'I know,' she said huskily, burying her face in his shoulder. She pulled away, her eyes meeting his for a long, silent moment. The emotion in his eyes made her want to cry.

Pete smiled, ruffling her hair. 'Go on, idiot—in you get!' He put her in the taxi and handed the driver a bunch of notes. 'Take the lady anywhere she wants to go.'

Louisa waved out of the back window as the car pulled away, and Pete stood waving back until she had disappeared into the distance.

It was only when he had gone that the tight knot of fear started to hurt her stomach. She felt suddenly sick with it. Jacey was not going to be pleased.

Jacey was going to kill her.

CHAPTER EIGHT

GREYSTONE House loomed up in front of her—silent, dark, laughing at her from behind its winged gables. Louisa shivered as she made her way along the path, feeling the shadows wrap around her, the air chill and silent as she stood waiting at the front door while she hunted in her bag for the spare key Jacey had given her.

When she opened the door she felt her nerves tauten. The heavy thud of the lock as it clicked back made her jump, and her knees were weak as she stepped over the threshold, closing the door behind her.

Then silence.

She stood listening, the knife edge of awareness making her stiffen. Jacey was here, somewhere. She could almost touch his presence. Her pulses leapt as she heard a movement in the dark hall.

'Where the hell have you been?'

The low, biting voice made her jump, pulses drumming hotly. Her eyes scanned the darkness, unable to see him.

'You left without me,' she said uncertainly. 'I couldn't find you.'

'You didn't try,' Jacey said under his breath.

The hair on the back of her neck prickled. 'I went to the car park, but you'd gone.'

The silence was laced with anger, and she could almost hear him breathing. 'How did you get home?' he asked. 'Taxi?'

154

'Yes,' she said, searching for his face.

There was a low growl of laughter that made her blood run cold. 'Radcliffe couldn't be bothered to drive you home afterwards?' he said tightly. 'Too tired after he'd had you?'

She saw his face suddenly. He looked demonic in the half light, the fleshless cheekbones reflecting what little light there was in harsh angles, his mouth tight and straight, uncompromising.

'I didn't go anywhere with Pete,' she said, heart pounding. 'He just helped me find a taxi.'

'It's almost three in the morning,' Jacey said tightly. 'Do you take me for a fool?'

'I forgot the time, I didn't realise——'

'No,' his lips curled back in a snarl, 'you didn't, did you? You forgot all about your husband, waiting for you. You went to your lover's bed for a few hours instead.'

The words shot like bullets from his mouth and she backed as he came for her, fear making her eyes wide, staring pools of liquid black.

'Please——' She put out her hands as he closed in on her, but his fingers were already sliding over her throat.

'That's good,' he muttered thickly. 'I like to hear you beg.'

His hands clamped her tight against him, and she felt the zip being pulled smoothly downwards, the silk dress falling from her body while she tried to catch it, pulling at it, but his hands took her wrists, pinning her to the wall.

'Don't, Jacey,' she whispered, her voice pulsing with fear and excitement. 'Nothing happened. We didn't make love.'

'Liar!' he muttered through clenched teeth, and

his mouth burnt on her throat as he pulled the dress down over her shoulders, exposing her breasts, his mouth moving closer to them, his tongue snaking out over her skin, making her tremble.

'Pete didn't touch me,' she protested, turning her head. 'He didn't!'

'Liar!' he bit out again, eyes leaping with rage.

He pulled the dress further, baring her to the waist, his hands running fiercely over her naked skin. He pressed her hard against him, kissing her ruthlessly until her legs weakened and she swayed, putting a hand out to steady herself.

'You went to him,' he muttered harshly, and pushed her down to the floor, kneeling over her. 'You went to *him*, you little bitch! Do you know how I felt when they told me where you'd gone?' His hands began unbuttoning his shirt, pulling at the buttons, his eyes gleaming in the darkness.

Panic made her act, scrambling to get up, her hands gripping the wall as she tried to stand. 'Don't . . .!' she cried breathlessly as he whipped her back to him, pinning her down with the length of his body.

'I wanted to kill you!' His mouth shook with rage as he bit the words out. 'I wanted to kill you, but it's all I can do to keep my hands off you. How do you make me feel like this?' he muttered hoarsely, his mouth burning on her throat. 'How do you make me hate like this?'

Her heart stopped as his mouth clamped over hers, draining her, clinging to her with a fierce heated passion that burnt way out of control. His body slid against hers, their flesh twining as he pulled his clothes off, breathing hard, the rough hair on his thighs making her twist restlessly, gasping against his shoulder.

He drove into her, his breath punched out in a cry as their bodies became one. 'Ah, Louisa . . .' he muttered, lying still, as though he couldn't move.

He was shaking, his whole body trembling. Then he moved, and they were clinging together, their hands feverish as they sought each other in the hot darkness, the only sounds those of their breathing, their hearts racing. Louisa clung to him, her mouth parted as she sought his, needing the fierce lovemaking, the ferocious, violent display of emotion. Their mouths met and clung as the spiral of excitement grew and she heard him breathing hoarsely against her mouth. Then she was gasping, shuddering against him as hot waves of pleasure made her convulse, clutching at him while he moved frenziedly with her until she heard the raw agony of his breathing as his fingers dug into her in the storm of a violent, pulsing climax.

The sound of his heart thudding was the only thing that broke the silence which followed. Louisa tried not to think as she lay in his arms, her own heart pulsing hotly throughout her body.

She wondered if Jacey really believed she had slept with Pete. It seemed incredible that he could. He must know she was in love with him, in spite of everything that had happened—she had married him, hadn't she? Surely he sees at least that much, she thought sadly.

How could he hope to hurt her if he thought she cared nothing for him? She trailed one finger across his shoulder blade, feeling the pulse that drummed hotly in his body, his skin warm and damp to the touch.

Suddenly he raised his head, looking down at her in silence. Then he rolled away, lying next to her, studying her intently as he rested his head on one hand, propped up by his elbow.

'I'm sorry,' he muttered. 'I lost my head.'

She raised her eyes to his, studying him thoughtfully. 'I know,' she said gently. 'I understand.'

He shot her an angry glance. 'You shouldn't,' he said, his eyes dark. The sooty lashes flickered against his damp cheek as he looked away in an uneasy silence.

Louisa watched him for a long time, then drew a deep breath and told him, 'Nothing happened between me and Pete. You have to believe that.'

'Do I?' he said with flat sarcasm, and it wasn't a question, it was a hard cold statement that meant nothing. He ran long fingers over his brow, smoothing out a frown. 'It's pretty difficult. You were all set to marry him a while back.'

'You could trust me,' she said gravely, studying him with unhappy eyes.

'Trust!' he said angrily. The dark eyes flicked to her and she saw just how angry he really was. 'When did you ever trust me, Louisa?'

She flushed, the words biting home. He was right, of course. When had she ever trusted him? And if she was honest, she would admit that he had given her everything he had, holding only certain things back from her.

'This has to end some time, Jacey,' she said through pale bloodless lips. 'We can't go on like this for ever.'

Jacey closed his eyes as though he couldn't bear to look at her any more. 'Go to hell!'

She stared at him, wounded. Watching him in disbelief, she felt her mouth tighten as the words sank home. Slowly she stood up, her body stiff as the pain echoed through her, numbing her, blotting out all thought. Gathering together the remnants of her clothes, she walked up the stairs to the peace and sanctuary of her room.

She went to apologise to Rizzio and Elizabeth next morning. The sun was struggling to rise above sulky grey clouds that hovered, glowering down at the world while the sun made little efforts to peep over them. Occasionally bright sunlight would stream across the crisp Yorkshire hills, only to be blotted out as the wind blew the clouds over it, sweeping grey shadows across the heather of the moors.

The house was in an uproar when she arrived. 'Guess who's here?' Elizabeth muttered when she opened the front door.

Louisa cocked an ear, listening to the guffaws of laughter inside, the howlings of Basil, and the loud music. 'I give up,' she said, smiling.

'Uncle Willy,' said Elizabeth irritably. She brushed back a clump of overgrown hair. 'And his poisonous little boy. Honestly, if he says "Can I have" once more, I'll boil him in oil!'

Louisa went inside, grinning. Basil galloped down the hall and knocked her flying, howling as he did so and lolloping all over her. She pushed him down firmly and turned to Elizabeth.

'I came to apologise about last night,' she said slowly. Watching the other woman, she wondered exactly what they had thought last night when she hadn't come back. 'I hope I didn't cause any trouble.'

Elizabeth's brows rose in straggly disorder. 'Not for us,' she said meaningfully. Pausing for effect, she added, 'Jason wasn't exactly thrilled about it, but that's not really any of my business, is it?'

Louisa looked away. She didn't need Elizabeth to tell her that Jacey had been absolutely livid.

Rizzio burst out of the living room. 'It's the bolter!' he said, grinning, and closed the door on a dreadful noise which emanated from within. Louisa wondered how many people were being murdered in there. 'Where did you get to last night, then?'

'Lost,' said Louisa, smiling as she looked at him. 'That's where I got to. I had to practically steal the Crown Jewels to pay for a taxi.'

There was a loud crash from the living room, and Elizabeth looked at Rizzio with loathing. 'I should have had you investigated before I married you,' she said irritably. 'One look at your loopy mother ought to have warned me!'

Rizzio rolled his eyes heavenwards and drew a halo over his head.

Louisa decided it was definitely time to leave. As far as Rizzio's family went, the skeletons were absolutely trooping out of the cupboards. Quickly she made her excuses to them and left, waving over her shoulder as Elizabeth watched her go from the doorway.

The sun smiled down on the back of her neck as she walked back to the house, and she suddenly felt a longing to be in London again. Being born and brought up in a city instilled a taste for noise in most people. It wasn't the bright lights that attracted, it was the pulse of a city like London, the noise of the traffic, the sound of taxis, the hurried pace of the people.

She looked around at the wildly beautiful Yorkshire moors and knew that although they were romantic, she would always be in love with London. It was in her blood.

Jacey was nowhere to be seen when she got back to the house. His car was still outside, so she knew he hadn't gone anywhere. Going into the kitchen, she began to make herself some coffee.

The back door opened, and she looked up to see him framed in the doorway.

'Where have you been?' he asked coolly.

He looked dangerously sexy in faded blue jeans and a crisp white shirt that showed off his deep tan beautifully. Louisa looked at his broad shoulders and wanted to touch him.

'Next door,' she told him. 'I went to apologise.'

'But not to me,' he drawled, his smile sardonic.

She flushed, putting down the cup she held. 'You didn't give me a chance. You just jumped down my throat.'

'Without reason, of course,' he said tightly.

She suddenly felt like smashing something over his obstinate head. 'You don't honestly believe I slept with him, do you?' she asked angrily.

His eyes narrowed as he watched her, and she felt her heart sink with disappointment. Obviously he did.

Jacey pushed his hands into his pockets. 'I don't know what to believe,' he muttered.

Louisa looked down at her hands in silence.

He gave an impatient sigh. 'What do you want from me, Louisa?'

She looked up angrily. 'Nothing,' she said

through tight lips. 'Nothing. Just forget it—forget the whole thing.'

His mouth hardened. 'Now look,' he said thinly, 'you knew what you were taking on when we married. I can't help the way I'm built. I'm a jealous guy, Louisa. When something like last night happens, my cool just flies straight out of the window!'

She laughed bitterly. 'Tell me about it!' she said through her teeth, with biting sarcasm.

Their eyes met and warred for a long tense moment. Louisa felt so angry she wanted to scream and break things. When she was at fault she could accept Jacey's violent temper—but when she hadn't done anything, she found it pretty difficult, to say the least.

His mouth was a firm angry line. 'I'm going out for a few hours,' he said in a clipped voice. 'I'll be back around three. Don't go out anywhere.'

She watched him slam out of the door and clenched her fists. However much he hated her, he was human, and a situation as emotionally volatile as their marriage would be intolerable to anyone. When would he stop, though?

Her anger dissipated into depression and she slumped against the wall, sighing. She remembered reading somewhere that Fitzgerald had said that in the depths of one's soul, it was always four o'clock in the morning. Fitzgerald knew too much, she thought irritably, staring at the wall with unseeing black eyes.

It was all to do with pride, of course. Jacey's pride was even greater than hers, but however powerful it was, it had to crumble under the weight of a need for understanding. And how could they ever understand each other if all they did was argue?

It was two o'clock when the car pulled up outside. Louisa frowned, going to the door. He was home early.

Her mouth dropped open. 'Pete!' she exclaimed in dismay, frowning as she looked past him to make sure Jacey wasn't around.

Pete's face was lined with strain as he studied her. 'Are you all right? He didn't hurt you last night?'

She put a hand to her head. It was just too unbelievable. How could he be so stupid as to come here today of all days? There he was, fiddling with a set of keys on the doorstep, and at any moment Jacey could come home.

Sighing, she opened the door wider. 'You can't stand there, someone might see you. Come in—but only for a minute.'

Pete walked in slowly, his spiky fair hair rippling in the breeze. He pushed it down with one hand. 'So what happened last night?' he asked, and Louisa saw the anxiety in his blue eyes as he watched her.

'Nothing,' she lied, avoiding his gaze. How could she possibly tell him the truth?

His thin brows jerked together. 'Nothing? Are you kidding? I've seen that guy, remember—and he's a nasty piece of work when he loses his temper.' He studied her intently. 'Do you expect me to believe he just laughed it off?'

Louisa drew a steady breath, pursing her lips. Pete had to accept that she really cared for Jacey, and until he did, he wouldn't come close to understanding her. He also had to try and forget her. No one knows what goes on inside a marriage, a partnership—any relationship, in fact—except the two people involved. And only a fool would try to interfere. It would be like putting a stick of dynamite under yourself.

'Look, you can't stay here, Pete,' she said quietly. 'If Jacey came back, he'd kill you.' She made a face, adding, 'And me.'

Pete's jaw clenched. 'So he did get nasty! Did he hurt you? Tell me, Louisa. If he did, I'll . . .'

'What?' she asked gently. 'Hit him?' She shook her head, eyes pained, 'Have you seen him lately? Even the Incredible Hulk would think twice!'

Pete reddened belligerently, and she bit her lip, wondering if she ought to have said that. But it couldn't be helped. She had to point the truth out to him or he wouldn't see it.

Then Pete sighed, kicking the floor with one worn trainer. 'I'm sorry,' he said under his breath, 'I guess I'm only in the way. I just wanted to help, that's all. I was worried for you.'

Louisa looked at his hurt eyes and felt like a complete bitch. 'Oh, Pete,' she said gently, 'I didn't want any of this to happen. I'd give anything to put it right—you know that.'

He gave her a little smile. 'Yeah,' he said, shifting restlessly. He jangled the keys in his hands. 'Why don't we go out for a drive? I promise I won't take you too far.'

Maybe that wasn't a bad idea, thought Louisa, and she nodded, smiling. 'Very well. But only for a while—he's coming home at three.'

The car was warm from the heat of the sun as they got into it. Louisa looked back at the house as they pulled away, and wondered why it always gave her the shivers. It looked so grim, even in sunlight.

'We're going back to London in six weeks,' Pete told her as they drove quickly along the narrow lanes. 'A new club's opened in Ilford, and we managed to get a booking. It should be all right—it's a lively place, not too far from the West End.'

Louisa smiled, thinking that marriage to Pete wouldn't have been so secure after all. She would have been tied to a life of travelling from town to town while he worked out his obsession with rock music. Her feelings for him were too platonic to live like that.

She herself was too intense in everything she did to be able to live without an obsession. At the moment, though, Jacey was consuming her. That both pleased and annoyed her. She wanted to be more than just his partner. She wanted to be herself—but she knew she wasn't complete without Jacey.

'Will you come and see us?' asked Pete, grinning.

She laughed. 'Steve would throw his drums at me!'

'No, he likes you, old Steve. He says you're a real hoot.'

She shook her head, murmuring, 'Where does he come up with these phrases?'

'You tell me!' Pete turned off the small road and began driving up a wider road. 'I sometimes think his only companions are ten-year-olds!'

Louisa sat up straight suddenly. They were driving on to a motorway. The wider road had been a slip road, and now they were joining the mainstream of traffic heading for London.

'What are you doing?' she asked, very still.

Pete threw her a determined look. 'I'm not letting you go back to him, Louisa. He's not good for you.'

She was speechless. A sign passed overhead with the word LONDON glaring at her in fluorescent white. She watched it in incredulity, frozen to the spot. He couldn't mean it!

'Turn off, Pete!' she exclaimed angrily as a sign indicating a slip road came up overhead.

He shook his head grimly. 'No way.'

'For heaven's sake!' she shouted. 'You can't be serious! He's my husband, Pete, and I'm not leaving him!'

Pete reddened, his face set like stone. 'I don't care,' he said mulishly, 'I won't stand by and see you hurt.'

She stared at him, frantic. 'Turn off this road, Pete!' But he carried on driving, and another slip road came up on their left. 'Damn you!' she shouted angrily, and reached for the wheel, grappling with him to turn the car left.

'What the——' Pete was horrified. The car careened and screeched all over the road.

The car behind them couldn't stop in time. It smashed headfirst into the side of Pete's car, knocking them with a sickening crash across the road.

Louisa didn't even have time to scream. Flung forward like a rag doll, she saw the world spin dizzily before her head thumped on the windscreen and blackness engulfed her like a yawning chasm.

She woke up in a surrealist world where everything was seen from a horizontal position. She was floating, lying down, an orange blanket thrown over her aching body. Heads bobbed around above her. The back of a St John Ambulance man was visible in front of her—and that was the moment she realised she was being carried on a stretcher.

It seemed perfectly normal to be lying down like a Roman empress while her bearers carried her.

'It's all right, love, we're taking you to the hospital,' said a broad Yorkshire voice and she looked up to see another man, strangely surreal, carrying her too.

She frowned, her head throbbing. 'I'll be late for work,' she told him, 'I have to get the bus.'

'That's right, miss,' said the man airily. 'Of course you do.'

It seemed perfectly normal to be loaded into the ambulance while the light flashed and whizzed. Louisa fingered the orange blanket, and wondered what she was doing here.

Then she remembered. 'Pete . . . where's Pete?' She sat up, putting a hand to her head as a stabbing pain hit right behind her ear.

'The driver?' asked the man who sat beside her. 'He got off lightly—just bruised and shaken.'

Sinking back with a sigh, she looked at her watch. Nearly three o'clock. Oh well, that's that, she thought, her mouth trembling. She suddenly felt weepy, and wanted to cry, but instead she lay still while the ambulance rattled tinnily away.

Ten minutes later she was being poked and prodded by a doctor who looked as though he should have retired twenty years ago. Peering at her, he doddered around, umming and erring to himself.

'Does this hurt?' he asked, his fingers biting into her leg.

'Yes,' she said through her teeth, wincing. She wondered what he would do if she poked him in the eye and asked the same question.

'Nothing serious, but there may be fractures,' the doctor said, and whisked her down to X-Ray where she was hauled into a dark green gown and poked and prodded some more. She felt utterly wrecked by the time she left the department.

They sat her in an uncomfortable chair in the waiting room where the sound of trolleys banging and nurses chattering was almost like piped music in a restaurant.

'Want a cup of tea, love?' asked a voice an hour later, and she looked up to see a voluptuous, middle-aged woman squeezed into a crisp white uniform.

'Please,' said Louisa, and the woman battered a tea trolley towards her, rolling up her sleeves as she poured the refreshing liquid into a chipped cup. 'How long do you think I'll have to wait?' asked Louisa as she was handed the tea.

The woman adjusted the cap on her dyed blonde head. 'Which doctor did you have?'

Louisa frowned. 'Doctor Masters, I think.'

'Oh dear!' The woman made a face, shaking her head. 'They get him out of his coffin every morning for surgery. I sometimes think that skeleton in his office is one of his patients, still waiting.'

That doesn't sound too promising, thought Louisa. Biting her lip, she wondered if Jacey was here yet. She had given her telephone number to a nurse on arrival. No doubt Jacey was waiting for her somewhere. She didn't dare think about what he would say when she finally appeared.

She was called back into the doctor's office, and told she could go home. Wagging a finger at her, the doctor told her how lucky she was, then told her to have a check up in three weeks' time in case anything was lurking unseen.

Jacey was waiting for her as the nurse led her out to the main waiting room, which was filled with harassed nurses and crying children, and which couldn't have done much to improve Jacey's temper.

'Here we are, Mr Knight.' The nurse handed her over with a professional smile, her eyes devouring Jacey. 'Right as rain, but a little shaken.'

'Poor darling,' Jacey murmured, studying Louisa from beneath hooded lids. His arm slid around her, his fingers splaying on her waist. 'How do you feel?'

She looked at him oddly, surprised by his calm greeting. 'I'm fine,' she said huskily, looking at him through her lashes, 'but my head hurts when I move it too far to the left.'

He leant her head on his shoulder, stroking her hair, and turned to lead her out of the hospital gates. The sun was bright as they walked to the car, the hospital gardens beautifully kept, the flowerbeds dazzling the eye with their bright array of colours.

They didn't speak on the way home, and Louisa glanced at his hard profile from time to time trying to decide whether he really was as calm as all that. The hospital must have told him where and how it happened.

When they pulled up outside the house, he

helped her out of the car, her head on his warm shoulder, and led her inside the house.

'You'd better rest,' he said coolly, and she felt that prickle of unease again as she studied him sideways. She could feel the deep regular beat of his heart through the thin white shirt, could feel the warmth of his flesh against her cheek.

As he laid her on the bed she looked at him through her lashes. 'I hope I haven't been any trouble,' she said quietly, her gaze intent.

'No trouble,' he drawled. 'At least Radcliffe didn't get away with it. I suppose we ought to be grateful for small mercies.'

Louisa flushed hotly, drawing an unsteady breath. She had been right to think he wasn't calm. He was like a volcano, seething with unleashed fire.

'I didn't realise what he was planning to do,' she muttered unsteadily.

'Of course not,' he replied, lips tight. 'That's why you'd got so far up the motorway.'

'I couldn't stop him . . .' she began, but he broke in with a barbed smile.

'Sure. He's just too strong-minded for you, isn't he?'

She looked at him miserably, seeing the old hatred creeping back into his eyes. 'Jacey, please——'

'You little bitch!' he grated through his teeth. 'You were leaving me!'

Her breath caught at the burning intensity in his eyes. 'No,' she said, shaking her head, 'I tried to stop him——'

'After everything I said . . . everything I did.' His lips curled back in a snarl. 'You must have laughed yourself sick this morning!'

She flinched from the violent tone. 'I didn't . . .'

'Shut up!' snapped Jacey under his breath, anger leaping from his eyes. He was breathing hard now, staring down at her. 'Were you going for good? Or was it just another moonlight flit?'

'Don't be so blind!' she said angrily, sitting up. 'I love you!'

His mouth shook with rage. 'Don't ever say that to me again,' he said between his teeth, and she whitened, incredulous.

'It's true!'

He looked down at her with contempt for a long moment. 'I'd like to kill you,' he said hoarsely, and for one split second Louisa thought he might. The black rage in his eyes was unmistakable. But instead he thrust her away from him. 'But why should I moulder in prison for a little cheat like you?'

He slammed out of the room and Louisa watched him go with a sob, her eyes brimming with tears of anger and frustration. She felt an overwhelming need to hit back at the injustice of it. Why had Pete done such a thing to her? He must have realised how much damage it would do. Hadn't she told him how she felt about Jacey? She had been trying to work towards a good relationship with him, and now it lay shattered at her feet.

Just when she was on the threshold of success, Pete had ruined everything, wrecked it beyond repair with one stupid, impulsive act.

She sighed, her lips tight. He hadn't acted out of malice. He'd only wanted to help her, had been worried for her. How could she possibly lay the blame at his door? In the end, she was the one to blame for wrecking all of their lives.

But what on earth was she going to do now? Good question, she thought grimly.

CHAPTER NINE

LATER that evening, Louisa heard voices from downstairs and recognised Rizzio and Elizabeth's penetrating tones as they spoke to Jacey in the hall. Their footsteps came up the stairs and advanced on her room, while Louisa waited quietly in bed until the door opened.

'Surprise!' called Rizzio, grinning as he popped his curly black head round the door.

Not quite, thought Louisa, but she smiled back all the same. They came inside, studying her closely, their eyes curious.

'Isn't she pale?' Rizzio said to Elizabeth as he looked at her. 'She looks like Nosferatu—one of the living dead!' He walked around the room like a zombie, arms stretched ahead of him, vacant expression on his face.

Louisa laughed, then clutched her head, groaning. 'Don't make me laugh, it hurts my head!'

Rizzio grinned, advancing on her, wailing hideously.

Elizabeth smacked his hand. 'Behave!' she warned, and turned to Louisa with a grimace. 'He's always like this post-Uncle Willy. It must be something contagious!'

Louisa smiled, leaning back against the pillows. She hadn't seen Jacey since he'd brought her home from the hospital. The silence had saddened her, but she knew there was little she could do about it.

'Why were you on the London road?' Elizabeth

asked, sitting down on the bed, studying her with a frown. 'Was Jacey with you in the car or something?'

Louisa held her gaze directly. 'I was on my own,' she said, hoping the subject would be dropped.

'Ah-ha!' Rizzio tapped his cheek with one long finger. 'Methinks there's something funny going on. Why should you be on your own on the way to London? You weren't running off, were you?'

Louisa felt herself flush hotly, and looked away. 'I was driving up there to visit a friend. I was coming back tomorrow,' she said, lying through her teeth on the spur of the moment. She hoped Jacey wouldn't tell them a different story.

Rizzio raised one dark brow. 'On your honeymoon?' he drawled.

Louisa fidgeted restlessly with the bedcovers. Luckily, at that moment the door opened, and Jacey came in with a tray of steaming hot coffee and four cups.

Louisa looked up. Their eyes met and she felt her mouth go dry.

'How do you feel, darling?' Jacey closed the door and came towards her with a tender smile.

She relaxed. At least he wouldn't let other people see the mess they had made of their marriage. 'Fine,' she said huskily.

He bent his head to kiss her. Louisa's hand curled over his brown throat, her pulses leaping, her mouth meeting his in a burning kiss. She drew a strained breath as he drew away, and stared into his eyes.

His gaze flickered over her body, seeing the way she strained towards him, her smooth breasts half exposed by the brief nightdress she wore. She felt his eyes burn into her flesh and shivered.

Elizabeth turned to Jacey as he set the tray down and poured coffee into the cups. 'What did the doctors say?'

Jacey handed her some coffee. 'It's nothing serious—just some cuts and bruises. I'll take her along for a check-up in a couple of weeks, see that everything's all right.'

Elizabeth nodded, and looked back at Louisa. She frowned, leaning over. 'That's a nasty cut,' she observed, scrutinising the wound on her head. 'Shouldn't you have something over that?'

Louisa shook her head. 'They said it would heal better uncovered.'

Unconsciously, she raised her fingers, running them gingerly along the jagged wound. It didn't feel as bad as she had thought it would. It was really a miracle that she had got off so easily. She could have been killed—they both could.

Rizzio and Elizabeth left after an hour, and Louisa sat in her room, listening to the sounds of their voices as they spoke to Jacey in the hall on the way out. She waited in a tense silence as she heard Jacey lock the doors, going from room to room. Then his footsteps came back upstairs, and advanced on her room. She listened and felt her whole body tense in alarm. Surely he wouldn't make love to her tonight?

The door opened, and his broad shoulders filled the doorway. Louisa's pulses drummed in her ears as their eyes met across the room.

'Goodnight,' Jacey said coldly, and she shivered at the icy expression in his eyes.

'Jacey . . .' she said huskily as he began to close

the door, and he stopped, looking across at her, his eyes cold.

'Well?' he asked flatly.

She swallowed, her throat tight. 'What's happening to us?' she whispered sadly.

His mouth tightened into a hard line. 'Goodnight, Louisa,' he said, and closed the door with a firm, resounding click. She slumped back against the pillows, too hurt to even cry. Some things just went too deep for tears.

She felt much better when she woke up next morning. Her head no longer ached, but her body was slightly weak, although not enough to make her uncomfortable. She showered in the blue bathroom and dressed in jeans and a white blouse before going downstairs.

Jacey was in the living room when she got downstairs. He looked up at her in silence, his face grim, and said absolutely nothing—his eyes said it all.

Louisa read the icy hatred in his expression and felt her heart hurt. Stiffly, she went out of the room again, unable to speak. It was finally over. There was no turning back any more. She had lost.

The doorbell rang and she froze. The silence in the hall was deafening as she stood rooted to the spot, unable to answer it for fear of who it could be. Then the door of the living room opened as the bell rang again.

'I'll answer it,' Jacey said grimly, seeing her white face.

She saw every muscle in Jacey's body tense as he opened the door to see Pete standing there. There was a very long silence as the two men stared at each other, aggression pouring out of them.

'What the hell do you want?' Jacey asked icily.

Pete looked past him to Louisa, his face obstinate. 'I came to see how she was. I was worried. After the accident, I didn't know what to do.'

Jacey laughed harshly. 'A little late, don't you think? You almost killed her, you realise?'

Pete whitened, his hollow face draining of colour. He looked at Louisa. 'Are you all right?' he asked huskily. 'I rang the hospital, but you know what they're like—they just told me they'd sent you home.'

She nodded sadly, seeing the anxiety in his eyes. Poor Pete! He hadn't meant any of this to happen. How could she blame him for caring about what happened to her? That was his only crime, after all.

'All right,' Jacey said in a tight drawl, 'now you've seen her, you can get out.'

Pete looked at him sharply, then drew a deep breath. 'I know what you're thinking——' he began, but Jacey broke in with a cutting smile.

'Oh? A bloody mind-reader now, are you?'

Pete flushed, pushing his hands in his pockets. 'Louisa didn't want to come to London with me. I told her we were going for a drive and then just went on the motorway.'

'Really?' Jacey said through his teeth.

Pete looked at him angrily, his mouth tightening. But he carried on regardless. 'That's how we crashed. She tried to grab the steering wheel and make me turn off the motorway, and a car smashed into us from behind.'

Jacey's face was murderous as he stared at him. 'You son of a bitch! You could have killed her!'

Pete glared at him. 'Don't you think I knew that? Don't you think I could . . .'

Jacey hit him. Louisa didn't see it coming. One moment they were standing snarling at each other, the next there was a sickening crack of bone as Jacey's fist shot out and slammed into Pete's jaw.

Louisa gasped, horrified, as Pete fell back against the porch door, clutching his chin and groaning. She ran to Jacey's side, not daring to comfort Pete because she knew that this was a test, a sort of milestone, and she knew that if she took Pete's side against Jacey, he would never ever forgive her.

Pete straightened, rubbing his jaw. He glared at Jacey, then looked at Louisa. 'You can't say I didn't try!' he said angrily, and ran a hand over his spiky hair. 'Goodbye, Louisa. I hope he's not as violent with you as he was with me!'

She watched Pete walk away down the path and felt very sad. She would have given anything at that moment to undo all the harm she had caused for all three of them. But what could she do?

Turning to look at Jacey, she felt her pulses leap with the crazy hope that Pete's words might have changed his mind, but studying his face, she saw no softening of his expression, no change in his eyes.

Jacey looked down at her. 'Satisfied?' he asked tightly, and walked away from her without another word.

She stared at his departing back in amazement, heard the click of the door as he went into the study and closed it behind him. Surely he didn't still think she'd been running off with Pete? Her fists clenched. It wasn't fair! What in God's name did she have to do to prove she loved him?

Enough was enough. Anger was boiling up inside her, suffocating her as she stood in the silent hall. How much more of herself did he expect her to throw in his path for him to walk over? There was only so much she could take—and she had taken it, right up to her back teeth.

She strode forward with a determination that surprised her. In all the time she had known Jacey, she had never felt so angry. How dared he push her into his shadow as though she was a piece of uninteresting silk?

Slamming the door back on its hinges, she stood in the doorway, mouth tight.

Jacey looked round, startled, then his mouth firmed. 'What do you want?' he asked curtly, pouring whisky from a decanter.

Her black eyes flashed. 'I want to smash something over your damned obstinate head!' she gritted through her teeth.

He gave her a barbed smile. 'Go ahead,' he drawled.

Her fists clenched. 'So clever, Jacey. But not clever enough to see what's right under your nose.'

He raised the glass to his lips, draining the whisky. 'Go on,' he drawled, 'I'm fascinated.'

'You'd better be,' she said tightly, 'because it's the only time you're going to hear it, so make the most of it.'

He observed her with narrowed eyes, then set his glass down on the table. 'Okay—shoot.'

She drew a deep breath. 'I've had enough. Enough of you, enough of the arguments—enough of the whole stupid business. I want it to stop—and I mean now.'

His mouth tightened. 'I'm not in the mood for hysterics——'

'*Hysterics?*' She was almost speechless, her teeth clenched as she stared at him. 'Hysterics? You swine! Our marriage is clattering down around our ears and you call it hysterics?'

Anger leapt into the green eyes. 'You pushed us into this,' he bit out, 'both of us. I asked you to wait for me, trust me—but no, you couldn't even do that, that was too much to ask.'

Louisa's temper hit the roof. 'You were married!' she shouted, eyes blazing. 'A married man running around with a twenty-year-old. What does that make you?'

His face was white, his eyes burning. 'A bastard,' he said thickly. He ran a hand through his hair, his fingers shaking. 'I know. Don't you think I'm ashamed of it?'

'You ought to be,' she said, breathing hard. 'I gave you everything, and you gave me sweet nothing.'

Hell blazed from his eyes. 'I loved you!' he said hoarsely. 'I couldn't let you go—but I couldn't tell you either. I was too scared of losing you altogether.'

Tears stung the back of her eyes and she blinked them back angrily, refusing to break down in front of him.

'Jacey,' she said in a broken voice, 'we have to solve this. You have to forget about me and Pete . . '

'*No!*' He slammed his hand on the table, eyes blazing, and Louisa jumped at the violence in his tone. He watched her, breathing hard. 'Never on this earth. I see the way he looks at you—do you think I'm blind? Do you think I'm inhuman?'

She started to shake with frustrated anger. 'Damn you! If you can't give me a chance, I'll leave you!'

Jacey went white. Louisa watched the colour drain from his face, leaving him as white as marble, the bones jutting out under his flesh as he stared at her in the tense silence that followed.

'You won't leave me,' he said under his breath.

She shook her head, furiously blinking back tears. 'What do you expect me to do? I don't want Pete—I want you. But you just keep on hurting me—how can you expect me to live like this?'

His mouth shook. 'You won't leave me!'

They stared at each other for a long moment. Then Louisa turned and walked to the door. She looked back, hoping he would try to stop her.

But he didn't move. He stood rigid, watching her walk out on him.

Call me back, she thought desperately, and turned once more to look at him. She searched his face, but all she saw was immovable, stony pride. Pride, she thought bitterly, and almost laughed. Pride was the culprit all along the line. For the rest of her life, she would never hate any emotion as much as pride.

The door closed with an icy finality behind her. Over, she thought as she climbed the stairs to her room, it's all over. She knew Jacey didn't want her to go—she had seen the look on his face, seen him whiten. But she couldn't back down now.

Pride again, she thought, and viciously hurled her clothes into her suitcase. If she was prepared to let him walk all over her, take over her true self, then she would be able to make their marriage work. But she just wasn't built to be a doormat. She'd rather die than have him wipe his muddy boots all over her back.

The hall was silent as she called a taxi from the nearest town. Looking towards the closed door of the study, she felt like smashing it down and breaking something over his obstinate head. He wouldn't come out, she knew that. He was too damned proud.

Like me! she thought, and laughed, tears in her eyes.

The taxi arrived and she handed the driver her case, looking back at the house. She wasn't sorry to see it go. It would always remind her of the arguments, the bad times with Jacey. She preferred to remember him as he was when she first met him. She bit her lip, swallowing on a sob.

'Where to, miss?' asked the driver.

She looked at him with glazed eyes. 'York Station, please.'

They were both at fault, she realised as the car drove along the narrow country lanes—Jacey because of his secrecy, and she, because of her stupid pride. She could hardly believe that it had all happened because she'd wanted to win a petty argument.

Well, she thought, what a lesson to be learned from that. Never let pride get in the way of your feelings.

She stopped dead, and her heart missed a beat as she sat very still. You fool!

'Turn the car around!' she said quickly, leaning forward.

The driver looked at her in the rearview mirror. 'What's that, miss?'

'Turn around,' she said breathlessly, 'I've changed my mind. I want to go home.'

He chuckled, 'Whatever you say, miss.'

Louisa, she thought, you're the biggest fool that ever lived. Imagine not seeing what was so glaringly obvious. The biggest mistake of her life had been caused by too much pride—and here she was, about to do it all over again, for the self-same reason.

She laughed aloud, tears blurring her vision as the house came into view. There it was, still grim and silent, but it didn't bother her this time. Jacey was in there, and that made it home.

She set her case down in the hall and walked slowly towards the door of the study. Taking a deep breath, she opened it.

Jacey looked up and she saw the raw agony in his eyes for one moment. Then he quickly masked it, looking away. 'What have you come back for?' he muttered under his breath.

Her throat stung. 'You,' she said, staring at him.

He looked up sharply, eyes narrowing. There was a very long silence, and Louisa found herself wondering if he could hear her heart beating, because she could feel it drumming through her body like a mad thing.

He sat quite still. 'What do you mean?' he asked deeply.

Tears spilled unchecked over her face. 'You,' she said huskily. 'I've come back for you. I love you, Jacey, I can't go on without you.'

He stood up slowly, his eyes never leaving her face. 'After all that's happened? After all I've done to you?'

She shook her head. 'I don't care.' Her lower lip jutted out, trembling, as she stared at him. 'I only want you. I only ever wanted you—you must know that.'

The silence seemed to stretch on endlessly between them, and she wanted him to move across to her, take her in his arms, but she knew he wouldn't move until he was sure, until he really trusted her.

'Radcliffe?' he asked deeply. 'What about him?'

Her mouth trembled. 'I was fond of him— nothing more. He was the brother I never had. I only wanted to marry him to hurt you, Jacey, to get back at you.'

His eyes were burning into hers. 'You knew I loved you. You knew I was jealous as hell. You must have known how much it would hurt me.'

She wiped at her tears with a shaking hand, her heart thudding. 'I was hurt too, Jacey.' She raised her eyes to his, her heart in them. 'I'm still hurting.'

Jacey drew a sharp, ragged breath at her expression, 'Louisa ...' He crossed the room, taking her in his arms, holding her close while she buried her damp face in his shoulder, breathing in the scent of him, feeling the warmth of his flesh, the unsteady thud of his heart. She was back where she belonged. With Jacey.

'How did it happen?' he whispered against her hair, stroking her head with tender fingers. 'It was so good, and then it fell apart before I could lift a finger to stop it.'

Louisa was shaking now, overwhelmed by the relief she felt. Nothing they had said to each other mattered now, so long as they were together again.

She didn't care that he had been married when they met—she knew he had loved her, still loved her, and all the wives in the world would have made no difference, because the feelings were more important.

'It was both of us,' she said huskily, rubbing her cheek against his shoulder. 'We should have been more honest with each other.'

He kissed her gently on the forehead. 'We were, at first. I thought I'd never known anyone so completely before. Do you know, I'd never opened up like that to anyone in my life. But when you came along, you changed everything.'

She knew what he meant. They had been closer than any couple deserved to be. But even knowing his soul hadn't made up for not knowing his background.

She sighed. 'There should never have been any secrets.'

His arms tightened around her. 'There never will be again,' he said deeply.

His mouth sought hers hesitantly, his kiss gentle, exploring as his fingers slid to her waist, holding her tighter against him. Then the kiss deepened and her heart raced, her pulses drumming like thunder as she slid her arms around his neck, clinging to him like a limpet, touching his hair with trembling fingers.

He drew away with a deep breath, studying her with eyes so tender she thought they might melt her.

'I love you,' he said huskily.

Louisa nodded 'I know,' her eyes locked into his, 'and I wouldn't leave here if the devil himself asked me to.'

'He just might,' Jacey murmured, lips against hers. 'We have to go back to London some time.'

'You,' she said with a smile, 'I take it, are the devil?'

'Who else?' He gave her a wicked smile, his eyes teasing. 'Why? Does that offend your sense of equality?'

'Anything you can do ...' said Louisa, grinning.

He groaned, holding her closer and murmuring over the top of her head, 'Why do I get the feeling I've married a feminist?' Then he held her away from him, frowning with amusement. 'You can't be, though. You gave up your job to marry me— no self-respecting feminist would do that.'

She wrinkled her nose. 'Rubbish! Feminism doesn't mean punching every man you see just because he's after your job. It means not putting up with any old stick from men just because they think they're better than you.'

He considered this with a thoughtful frown. 'I never met a man who thought he was better than me.'

Louisa's cheeks dimpled. Then her gaze fell on his mouth and she felt her heart skid crazily. Inches from her own, his lips were firm, sensual, and her pulse raced as she strained against him.

'Are we just going to stand here all night?' she asked throatily, and slid one hand along his brown throat, feeling her mouth go dry.

Jacey's heartbeat thudded faster. 'I thought we should celebrate,' he said smokily, eyes resting on her mouth. 'What would you like to do?'

She slowly raised her eyes to his, clinging to him. 'Can't you guess?' she whispered.

He drew in his breath as he met her gaze. 'I like a lady who knows what she wants,' he said thickly.

'Oh, I do,' she murmured, and proceeded to demonstrate.

THE MYSTICAL ISLE OF MAN

It is little wonder that Sarah Holland has been inspired to write such delightful romances as *Tomorrow Began Yesterday* (Presents #536) and *Fever Pitch*. For Sarah Holland, a comparatively new Harlequin author, lives on the Isle of Man, a mystical romantic place of inspirational beauty and folklore in the Irish Sea.

First settled by the Celts, then conquered by the Vikings, the Isle of Man owes its romantic atmosphere to these ancient founding races. On a tour of the thirty-mile-long island it is not unusual to come across the remains of their round dwellings, runic crosses and monuments. Even the Celts' lilting language, which is related to Gaelic, is still spoken by a few Manx, as the residents are called. But perhaps the best legacy from the past are the stories of the island's magical inhabitants, the "little people," of whom there are two types: the *phynnodderee*—the wicked little people—recognized by their hairy faces and bright eyes; and the *mooinjer-ny-gioneveggey,* the good little people. Usually dressed in green with red caps, the latter can be found dancing in glens or splashing in waterfalls. Their benevolent nature, however, lasts only until someone does them insult or injury, such as calling them fairies, a term these sturdy little folk especially scorn.

Perhaps Sarah might one day give us the pleasure of setting a romance on this mystical island!

Take these 4 best-selling novels FREE

ANNE MATHER
born out of love

VIOLET WINSPEAR
time of the temptress

CHARLOTTE LAMB
man's world

SALLY WENTWORTH
say hello to yesterday

Harlequin Presents...

Take these 4 best-selling novels FREE

Yes! Four sophisticated, contemporary love stories by four world-famous authors of romance FREE, as your introduction to the Harlequin Presents subscription plan. Thrill to **Anne Mather**'s passionate story BORN OUT OF LOVE, set in the Caribbean.... Travel to darkest Africa in **Violet Winspear**'s TIME OF THE TEMPTRESS ....Let **Charlotte Lamb** take you to the fascinating world of London's Fleet Street in MAN'S WORLD .... Discover beautiful Greece in **Sally Wentworth**'s moving romance SAY HELLO TO YESTERDAY.

Join the millions of avid Harlequin readers all over the world who delight in the magic of a really exciting novel. EIGHT great NEW titles published EACH MONTH! Each month you will get to know exciting, interesting, true-to-life people .... You'll be swept to distant lands you've dreamed of visiting .... Intrigue, adventure, romance, and the destiny of many lives will thrill you through each Harlequin Presents novel.

Harlequin Presents... The very finest in romance fiction

Get all the latest books before they're sold out!

As a Harlequin subscriber you actually receive your personal copies of the latest Presents novels immediately after they come off the press, so you're sure of getting all 8 each month.

Cancel your subscription whenever you wish!

You don't have to buy any minimum number of books. Whenever you decide to stop your subscription just let us know and we'll cancel all further shipments.

Your FREE gift includes

Anne Mather—Born out of Love
Violet Winspear—Time of the Temptress
Charlotte Lamb—Man's World
Sally Wentworth—Say Hello to Yesterday